"I don't even kno
fictional characters."

JJ's hand rested on the doorknob of her office door. After her second cup of coffee, the pounding in her head quit and she found she was able to stand and walk. She was ready to retire to her bedroom for the night.

"Wow, 'fictional characters' make us sound so," Blake paused a beat, "unreal." He pinched himself in the forearm. "Ouch. See, that hurt me. I'm real."

"But you're not real. You're just personalities I created. You're nothing more than flat two-dimensional characters in a love story—the love story I created. You are not real."

JJ heard Alex softly sniffle and glanced at her heroine. Her eyes were tearing up. She sighed and fought back the urge to walk over and comfort her. *She's not real.*

"So, that could only mean one thing," she said, as if to reinforce that thought, "I'm talking to myself right now." She threw her hands into the air.

JJ turned the doorknob but paused for a brief moment. "In the morning, I'll realize this was all a dream." *Or a really bad hallucination.*

"I'll walk in tomorrow and my office will be empty. It will be quiet and serene." She glanced at the pair. "Goodbye."

And with that, she walked out, closed the door behind her, and headed straight for bed.

JODY!

ENJOY

Terry Newman

Rewrites of the Heart

by

Terry Newman

Rewrites of the Heart

Cover Art by *Kristian Norris*

The Wild Rose Press, Inc.
PO Box 708
Adams Basin, NY 14410-0708
Visit us at www.thewildrosepress.com

Publishing History
First Edition, 2023
Trade Paperback ISBN 978-1-5092-4653-3
Digital ISBN 978-1-5092-4654-0

Published in the United States of America

Dedication

This book is dedicated to my daughter, Marie.
For so many reasons.

Chapter 1

"Good morning, sunshine."

That voice, even muffled, indistinct, and distant, sounded eerily familiar. Yet, JJ couldn't quite place it. Had she imagined it? She held still a moment, as she tried to decide where she had heard it before.

Silence.

Shifting her weight, she snuggled her head deeper into the pillow of her crossed arms on the desk, rolled her chair about a bit, finding the perfect position and posture. Then, sighing deeply and contently, she prepared for the return of sleep.

As she floated in the dream-like world between sleep and wakefulness, she sensed she must have dozed off while working on her novel. Perhaps my sister is right, she thought, maybe I am working too hard. This was becoming a habit.

Nobody was calling her. Nobody needed her. She wrapped herself in the comfort of peaceful slumber. The manuscript could wait a little longer. All she needed was a few more minutes of glorious rest…and then…

"No use ignoring us."

The voice cracked the silence like a hammer hitting a slab of ice. The words jolted her awake. She sprung into a full sitting position. It was the same voice again. She was sure of it. Only now it sounded closer than before, sharper, more commanding.

Another moment of silence—this time not so peaceful. She felt goose bumps run up her arms at the thought someone might actually be talking to her. She lived alone. How could anyone be calling her? Tension and fear paralyzed her. She tried to move an arm but couldn't.

"We're not going anywhere."

She tried to blink away the blurred surroundings, to focus her eyes on her home office. She could feel the rhythm of her heart increase as it beat faster. The echoing of it in her chest vibrated with panic and pulsed through her body. Could it be she wasn't alone?

She blinked several times more. It was difficult to focus. Last night's long hours still fogged her thoughts. The scenes and the characters of her novel still dancing, center stage, through her head.

Her sense of reality languidly returned. Cobwebs stubbornly clung to the innermost recesses of her mind. She sat completely still for a moment longer, unnerved by the very possibility that someone was watching her.

Then slowly, eyes finally adjusting, she scrutinized her surroundings. She carefully surveyed the eclectic mix of elements that made this office a welcoming work room for her. The mahogany bookcase against the far wall, filled with college history books and romance novels. The photos of her late husband and herself mounted above the credenza made her smile. She glanced at the man and woman on the loveseat blithely staring at her, before she turned her attention to the large pile of papers on her desk.

A couple sitting on her loveseat? Was that right? Her eyes immediately shot back to the pair. She gazed at them for what seemed like an eternity but was merely a few seconds.

"It's about time you acknowledge our presence," the man said.

She let out a blood-curdling scream and shot up out of the chair like a rocket, the full impact of what she saw finally hitting her. The stack of papers scattered about the room like huge dandelion seeds on a windy day. The chair clunked down, falling to one side.

She couldn't get out from behind the desk quickly enough. "W-w-who are you? How did you get in here?" She also wanted to know why they were drinking from her favorite coffee mugs, but that seemed far less the issue at the moment.

The man spoke first. "Why, you were right, love," he said, directing his remarks to the woman sitting to his left. "She doesn't recognize us."

The young woman just smiled and sipped her beverage. Swallowing slowly, her gaze caught JJ's. Then she looked at her companion. "Well, Blake, it's not every day characters like us drop in out of the blue."

The woman crossed her legs, lightly tugged at her red dress, and glanced back at JJ with a smile that was so disarming she had to fight the urge to smile back.

"It really is a shame."

"Indeed, Alex, you would think that she would know us instantly, now, wouldn't you?" They continued to talk between themselves, purposely and calmly, ignoring her presence.

"No," she said, "I don't recognize you two because I don't know who the hell you are or how the hell you got into my house."

"But we know you." The gentleman brought the cup to his lips but paused before sipping. "You're JJ Spritely, the romance author."

"H-h-how do you know me?"

Fearful of making any sudden moves, she slowly inched toward the telephone on the desk, ensuring she was within a hand's reach of it. Instead of reaching for its receiver, though, she reached down, toward her foot.

She struggled to gain her composure and try to direct her mind to work. She felt as if her brain were scattered along the better part of two states. She wondered how she would defend herself if they were dangerous. She had read that high heels made an effective weapon. What was she wearing? Bunny slippers. She couldn't hurt anyone in those things. When was the last time anyone had been "fluffed to death"? Still, she was hesitant to make any quick moves, not knowing what these two characters wanted.

"I'm Blake," the man said flatly, as if that name should mean something to her. "Blake Teesdale."

"And I'm Alex. Alex Zurich. Remember me?"

JJ leaned her head forward, scrutinizing the pair. "Oh. My. God. You're not. You couldn't be."

The last thing she heard before she fainted was the man who called himself Blake say, "Didn't see that one coming, did you, Alex?"

Chapter 2

JJ woke up nearly eyeball to eyeball with the self-proclaimed fictional heroine of her novel. She squealed, startling the other woman, who let out a squeal of her own.

Note to self: Don't shriek. Head pounds worse. She felt as if someone had pumped her head full of helium to the point where it would stretch past its limit and burst at any minute.

Nervously, she squirmed backward trying to put as much distance as possible between the alleged heroine and herself. But she couldn't go far. It was at that point, she realized she was lying on the loveseat.

Oh, it's all coming back to me now. She glanced around. She was still in her office. The man who claimed to be the hero from her book had been pacing directly behind his partner. With arms extended behind his back, head down, staring at the carpet, he determinedly walked back and forth while the female stood guard over her. The cries jolted him out of his reverie, and he strode over.

"I'm sorry," the dark-haired beauty said, now kneeling in front of the sofa. "We never intended to scare you like that."

The man apologized as well. Gingerly, he sat on the arm of the couch and took her hand. "Never expected you to keel over like that, love."

"We didn't think you'd mind if we just jumped out

of the novel you had us in and pop in on you while you dozed a bit," he said. "We knew you were working on our love story just about nonstop, and you know we adore your devotion to us and all, but you really need to kick back some and take care—"

"Blake." Alex reached up and lightly slapped him on the shoulder. She looked him squarely in the eyes.

Even in JJ's befuddled state, she could clearly recognize the love and dedication this woman had for her hero. The way she gazed into his large, chocolate brown eyes told the whole story.

"Oh, I'm sorry," Blake said, "but we really did want to be there when you woke up." The heroine nodded vigorously.

"You see, you've taken such good care of us the last couple of months," she said, continuing her partner's train of thought. She ran her hand through her thick, dark brown hair, as if she were searching for the right words. The long hair fell to one side. JJ swore she heard Blake whimper.

"You've spent so much time and effort developing our characters, making sure our lives were on the right track, keeping us from taking the wrong turn in the road, so to speak, that we wanted to return the favor to you."

"Some favor, huh? Making you keel over in a dead faint? Just what kind of grateful characters are we, anyway?" Blake looked sincerely apologetic—and handsome. No wonder Alex fell in love with him so hard, she thought. *That is if these two were really from my novel. Which is totally impossible. But if that's not who they are, who are they?*

JJ took a deep breath, then exhaled. She thought, maybe, she was experiencing some existential meltdown. But since she wasn't quite sure what existentialism was, she couldn't be sure.

On the surface, it appeared the main characters from her current work in progress were standing in her office. For apparently no good reason. Not that an obviously good reason for them being there would make it easier to understand.

She felt the two staring down at her. A bit unnerving to say the least. She slowly sat up. "Be careful," the female cautioned. "You were out for a while." Attempting to stand, JJ quickly determined it was beyond her capabilities, at least for the moment. She sat, closed her eyes, and sighed deeply.

What kind of trick is my mind playing on me? She opened her eyes again and scrutinized the man who said he was Blake Teesdale, the hero from her book, *Love's Surprise.*

At six feet, he certainly fit the bill. He had black, wavy, unruly hair that danced wildly from side to side as he talked. The more animated his speech, the wilder his hair jostled about his tanned, ruggedly handsome face. And the more passionate he appeared on the topic at hand, the more his hair bounced.

It really didn't matter what he talked about, she recalled from the description she had painted of him, he was passionate about everything. And that was the trait that initially drew Alex Zurich to him. Now, it was coming back to her. The heroine also loved the man because he could make her laugh.

And Alex, well, she was beauty personified. JJ liked to think she endowed her with every good quality she personally lacked. She also envisioned this fictional character as a classic beauty—something that no one had ever accused her of being.

JJ took another look at her. At nearly five foot nine inches, the woman had a small waist, slender hips, and was well-endowed. Just enough to make her extremely attractive and mildly seductive. All of this was set off by her long, shapely legs which were seldom hidden by a pair of jeans. In so many ways, she was a throwback to the 1940s pin-up model.

If men were initially attracted to her because of her body, they were equally as intrigued by her face. Her hair framed green eyes that flashed when she was angry but sparkled like expertly cut emeralds when she laughed.

Now that she looked at them in more detail, JJ realized she did know them. Why, of course, they were creations of hers, even though she couldn't explain how they came to be standing in front of her.

"I smell coffee," she said, slowly emerging from her fog-like state. "Is there any left? I could really go for a cup right about now." *Actually, I could use a stronger type of beverage, but coffee will have to do.*

"Oh, yeah, there's a quite a bit left," Blake said, his voice brightening up a bit. "I'll get you a cup."

"I didn't know you drank my favorite coffee blend. French roast." JJ could hear Blake close a kitchen cabinet door. "What a coincidence."

Letting her guard down some, she couldn't help but smile as she answered. "Why do you think it's your favorite?" *What am I saying, talking to him like he's really from my book?*

Blake entered the room and handed her the cup, then leaned casually against her desk so he was across from her.

"Quite clever. Quite clever," he commented.

Alex positioned herself next to JJ on the sofa.

JJ took the coffee and tried to lift an eyebrow like she had some of her favorite characters do. But they refused to work independently of each other. She had to settle for communicating with words. "How so?"

"Most people, upon discovering I'm English, naturally assume I drink only tea. But no, you break that stereotypical mold and make me an avid coffee lover. Touché."

With some hot java circulating through her system, she could feel that helium in her head dissipating. The violent pounding eased. As her head cleared, she relaxed a bit. Surprisingly, she was beginning to feel quite at ease with these two intruders—whoever they were.

Then Alex evidently decided it was time to raise the real reason for their visit in a little more detail. She turned her body, so she faced JJ.

"Can't you see you two were made for each other?"

"Of course," the Englishman agreed.

JJ swiftly looked in Blake's direction as she attempted to make sense of the conversation.

"Think of the encounter as a scene from one of your novels. All you need to do is kiss him, jump him, and get on with the good part of the relationship."

At that, she gagged and spit out her coffee. Alex glared at him.

"What?" he said, seemingly innocently. "I was only agreeing with you."

"What he's trying to say is that your chance meeting sounds exactly like something you'd write in one of your novels. And you know darn well that if you had written this, and you weren't the main character of this episode, as you are, the two of you would be approaching a love scene by now."

She looked at them blankly. "And just who and what are you talking about?"

"Why Professor Kennedy King Cooper, of course. And don't try to tell me you don't remember him. You have to be totally out of it not to take note of a hunk like him."

She was so stunned by the subject of the conversation, she didn't even question how they knew about this dismal episode in her life. She hurriedly countered their amazingly stupid suggestion. The audacity of these two.

That man was the most ill-mannered, arrogant... She stopped herself in mid-thought and turned toward Alex before she continued.

"Oh, come on. You mean that man in the bookstore? I'll never see him again. And thank goodness for that. He's a sexist, elitist egotist."

"You liked him that much," Blake mumbled. Alex nudged him in the ribs.

"What?"

Chapter 3

JJ shook her head as she thought about that incident. She remembered it as if it happened yesterday. Wait, it was yesterday.

The "encounter" had started innocently enough—but then these things always did. Somehow, it had snowballed into a series of totally inane incidents. Before she knew it, she found her career being attacked by a total stranger. Granted, a handsome total stranger.

And in some ways, she thought wistfully, it really was a shame. For the first few moments of their meeting, she did feel that special spark she made sure her heroines experienced. In fact, if she didn't know better, she might say she was sexually attracted to him. That's silly, though. You can't be drawn to a man you don't even know. That sort of emotion is, well, for the pages of fiction.

She had bumped into him—literally—at a book signing at the local bookstore, *A Likely Story.* After nearly an hour of nonstop smiling and autographing, JJ finally slipped away to browse the shelves. She naturally drifted to the history section of the store, being a former history professor herself.

Her eyes became laser beams as they locked onto all the new releases she'd missed the last several months since she'd buried herself in her fictional world. She wasn't paying attention to where she was walking. And she walked right smack dab into him. Embarrassed, she looked up at him (her five-foot-two-inch height always seemed to put her at a disadvantage). She apologized but couldn't help notice that he was not only good looking but radiated a definite sensual aura.

He was tall, but, heck, everyone appeared tall to her. She guessed he was five-foot-ten, but she wouldn't have been surprised if he were six-foot. His dark brown hair was so meticulously coifed, she couldn't help but wonder if he were a news anchor.

His angular facial features, square jaw, and aquiline nose were features that could appear harsh and craggy if viewed separately. But when combined, though, it created an alarmingly handsome appearance.

His smile revealed creases around his sepia-brown eyes that hinted, JJ thought, at an innate boyish charm. If she were creating a hero for a novel, she would model the character after him.

It felt as if someone had trickled ice water down her spine as she took a step away from him. Then almost instinctively she checked what she was wearing. She couldn't remember.

She wore, as was her custom for a professional appearance, her most conservative clothes. White button-up blouse, men's cut, buttoned rather high and a brown jacket thrown over a pair of nice, but not overly tight jeans. Wouldn't you know it?

When she dressed that morning, she thought she presented a tastefully refined appearance. Now there were only two words she used to describe her appearance: Dowdy. Frumpy. And, yeah, ten years older than her actual age. Okay, so that was more than two words. She stopped there, even though she could have continued in that vein for a while.

Just my luck, she thought, bedraggled ex-history professor meets hunk at bookstore. Hunk yawns, excuses himself in a panic, and breaks the sound barrier running in the opposite direction.

Surprisingly, he didn't run. Instead, he struck up a conversation. They chatted politely about history. It seemed like the obvious topic with World War II flashing at them from the shelves and the Civil Rights movement towering before them. Then he made a remark about the book signing. She listened, amused, and then she slowly became irritated as he rambled on about the absurdity of the "trash" of romance novels (his exact words, she recalled).

"It's refreshing to see a woman who appreciates the finer points of an education," he told her, "and doesn't stoop to reading such mindless garbage. Only a hopelessly mindless bimbo would read that stuff. And I couldn't imagine what type of woman would actually lower herself to such depths to write that drivel."

Just at that moment, as fate would have it, a fan walked up to her.

"Excuse me, Ms. Spritely, I hate to bother you, but the clerk said you wouldn't mind. Would you please sign my copy of *Love's Revenge*?"

She smiled, retrieved all the details needed for the autograph, chatted for a few moments with her fan, and then turned back to the gentleman. "And you were saying?"

The man's jaw hung open wider than the entrance to a cavern. She, however, glowed.

"Yep, that's me," she said. "And by the way, you know what this hopelessly mindless bimbo—those were your words, weren't they?—did before she became a fulltime author?" She paused for the sole purpose of creating a dramatic moment.

"This bimbo was a history professor." She abruptly turned on her heel, smiling broadly as she headed for the in-store café. She bought her favorite coffee, a caramel mocha, grabbed an asiago pretzel as a treat, and went back to her seat at the book signing table. *Oh, yeah. Life was good.*

Later, the man stopped by the booth to apologize. She smiled graciously. Her thoughts, though, were anything but gracious. What a waste of a sexy, attractive body. It's stuck in the mindset of an arrogant Neanderthal. Just my luck, she thought. To meet a guy with some chemistry to him—and even similar interests—only to find he's not just the proverbial frog, but the pompous ass as well. *And that's my modern fairy tale.*

"May I make this up to you?" he offered. He had asked for her phone number, but she declined to give it to him. Not to be brushed aside quite so easily, he handed her his business card. "Kennedy King Cooper, Professor of History, University of Northern Ohio." She read it briefly.

"If you should like to go for coffee some time and help me remove my foot from my mouth, I'd be grateful."

She held the card for a moment, almost tempted to take it. He did look attractive there in a boyish sort of way, part pouting, part pleading for a second chance on making a first impression. And, yes, she really did feel some type of attraction to him, pompous ass or not. But something told her not to take the card. She politely handed it back to him.

"No, thank you. I don't think we have much more to talk about." Thankfully, an individual with a book to sign walked up, signaling the end of the conversation.

"But he didn't mean to be such a sexist, elitist egotist, JJ." Alex pleaded the professor's case for him. "Remember the absolute bozo Blake was when I first met him? And we overcame it."

Blake's eyebrows scrunched together, his lower lip jutted out as he quietly muttered, "Bozo? I was a bozo?"

Alex calmly shook her head and took his hand. "You were a loveable bozo, honey."

The characters' banter shook her out of her reverie, and she discovered they were peering at her, apparently still expecting an answer.

Lowering her voice to almost a whisper, she said with a controlled anger, "He came off as a perfect pompous ass."

Chapter 4

"I made a perfect pompous ass of myself." Kenn stared trance-like into his cappuccino. He sat across from his college roommate, Rob Jenson, in a booth at the Physics Café, just off the campus of the University of Northern Ohio.

"I did try to make amends by offering her my card. But it was futile to think after that encounter she would call me."

"Where did you meet this woman?" Rob asked as he swirled the coffee in his cup.

"At the bookstore. I saw her out of the corner of my eye. We accidently bumped into each other in the history section. For a fleeting moment, I thought I may have found the woman of my dreams, beautiful and fiery."

He took the last sip of his coffee. "I just didn't know how fiery she was."

"What happened?" Rob asked.

"I said something about admiring women who liked history. But I went a bit too far in my compliment."

Rob raised his eyebrows. He took that as a sign to continue his story.

"I had seen a table set up for some romance novelist who was doing a book signing. So, I wondered out loud why any woman would read romance novels, let alone write them. That's when I found out she was the author signing those books."

Rob gagged and spewed coffee all over the table. He coughed and placed his napkin over his mouth.

"You okay?"

Rob nodded yes, then finally managed to speak. "You say she was the novelist?"

"Yeah. I was pretty blunt in my opinions," Kenn said, as he wiped the table. "It's sad, because if my mouth hadn't worked faster than my brain, I may have had a real chance to get to know her."

He paused. "But then again, why would I want to know a woman who writes such utter nonsense?"

"Kenn, why don't you come over to dinner one night? Nan knows some really nice women who would be perfect for you. A nice, friendly atmosphere, no pressure."

"Not that again." Kenn laughed. "I remember the last woman you introduced me to. What were you thinking? We had absolutely nothing in common."

"This time, I'm thinking about one person in particular. I think you two would get along really well."

"Thanks, but I think I'll pass." Kenn looked into the cup.

The conversation turned to other matters. Finally, Kenn said, "I better stop at the office before heading home. Thanks for listening."

As they left the café, Rob said, "Remember, Nan has lots of friends. You've got a standing invitation for dinner."

"Thanks. I'll keep that in mind."

Chapter 5

"I don't even know why I continue to argue with two fictional characters."

JJ's hand rested on the doorknob of her office door. After her second cup of coffee, the pounding in her head quit and she found she was able to stand and walk. She was ready to retire to her bedroom for the night.

"Wow, 'fictional characters' make us sound so," Blake paused a beat, "unreal." He pinched himself in the forearm. "Ouch. See, that hurt me. I'm real."

"But you're not real. You're just personalities I created. You're nothing more than flat two-dimensional characters in a love story—the love story I created. You are not real."

JJ heard Alex softly sniffle and glanced at her heroine. Her eyes were tearing up. She sighed and fought back the urge to walk over and comfort her. *She's not real.*

"So, that could only mean one thing," she said, as if to reinforce that thought. "I'm talking to myself right now." She threw her hands into the air.

JJ turned the doorknob but paused for a brief moment. "In the morning, I'll realize this was all a dream." *Or a really bad hallucination.*

"I'll walk in tomorrow and my office will be empty. It will be quiet and serene." She glanced at the pair. "Good bye."

And with that, she walked out, closed the door behind her, and headed straight for bed.

A quick glance at the alarm clock on her nightstand told her it was midnight. Of course, the witching hour. All sorts of strange things are said to happen at midnight. At the moment she couldn't think of any, but she knew she was right.

Kicking off her bunny slippers, she climbed straight into bed. She pulled the blanket close around her neck, cocooning herself under the covers, feeling its comfort and warmth. She thought this was what a caterpillar must feel as he slept snugly inside his chrysalis.

She smiled at the thought but knew full well the fundamental difference between her and the caterpillar. When the caterpillar awakes, he'll be a beautiful butterfly. *When I wake up tomorrow morning, I'll be the same old me.* Then, she quickly added, minus the two fictional characters in the office.

Of course, it'll be that way. She sighed. That whole episode was nothing more than a bad dream. At most, she thought, a hallucination brought on by too much work.

Maybe my sister is right. The thought reverberated through her head again. JJ's mind wouldn't shut down and refused to let her sleep.

Maybe I do work too much and maybe I'm not living my own life. Could it really be that I'm trying to live through my characters, as Nan claims?

The thought wouldn't leave her. *When they become real enough to me that I imagine I'm interacting with them in my office maybe it is time to ease up just a bit.*

Now, JJ's mind went full speed ahead like a car careening out of control. She knew she was treading icy water, but her thoughts naturally drifted toward the recent past. She couldn't help but reflect on the last four years. It hadn't been easy for her. But she was determined to continue on with her work, to carry on with her career. That's what Geoff would have wanted.

Geoff was Geoff St. Clair, her late husband. He died four years ago. Valentine's Day. Killed in a car accident. The same day the publisher released her first novel. After all the encouragement he provided her, tears of frustration he wiped away, and endless drafts he patiently waded through and edited, he never actually saw a book of hers in print.

If it wasn't for Geoff, she never would have had the courage to walk away from a burgeoning academic career. She never could have made the move from history professor to novelist.

At that moment, she felt like the widow she was. Too young to be a widow, someone told her at Geoff's funeral. But that didn't change the facts. Indeed, at twenty-eight she was one.

She fell asleep imagining how different her life would be if only her husband were still alive and rooting for her success.

Chapter 6

JJ got out of bed the following morning feeling much better. *Silly me, I couldn't have really believed the characters from my book had visited. It's like a bad take on* A Christmas Carol. *Scrooge had his three ghosts warning him. I have two of my own creations "haunting" me over a meeting with some jerk.*

Bleary-eyed, she put a robe and her fluffy bunny slippers on and padded to her study. It was five a.m.; she was already running behind her usual four o'clock start. But, as soon as she opened the door, she knew something was horrifically wrong. They were back.

Alex, sitting at the computer, leaped straight up like a startled cat when she walked in. Blake, totally absorbed in reading a book from her shelves, didn't flinch.

"You guys back? I thought we settled things yesterday. What gives?"

That comment prompted Blake to look up from the book. "What do you mean 'back'? We never left."

"Why not? I believe your work here is done."

Alex shook her head as she got back into the chair. "Apparently not. We can't return to our story. I don't think we're going anywhere anytime soon."

She pulled Alex out of the chair and settled into it. As she called up her manuscript, she was determined to act as if nothing was out of the ordinary. "You mean I'm stuck with you two for a while?"

"Hey, I resent that." Blake's lower lip jutted out slightly. "You created us, and you don't even want to spend time with us? Should we be insulted?"

The writer sighed. She rubbed the back of her neck. Too early, she thought, for a tension headache. Twenty-four hours ago, life seemed so easy.

She woke up in the morning, wrote for five to eight hours, ran errands in the afternoon, and then came home, watched television, or whatever else she wanted to do. After all, she lived alone. No dog to walk. No cat to deal with. Not even a goldfish to remember to feed. She had grown accustomed to her single existence.

She reflected on her first year of living alone. It took her that long to come to grips with her husband's death. She recalled that heartbreaking period. The times she turned to talk to him, then abruptly remembered he wasn't there. Running out of her office to tell him she had finished a book, then realizing… The void in her heart that couldn't be filled.

She shuddered. She really didn't want to revisit that pain. She had been with Geoff for far too short a time. She feared if she dwelled on those days, she would relapse into the deep, dark depression she had experienced after his death. She pushed all that aside.

Instead, she focused on the moment. She accepted her time alone now (or so she kept telling herself). It hadn't been easy. In fact, some days, it proved to be a real battle. The pain, though, gradually subsided.

She reminded herself of all the advantages to her new life. She came and went as she pleased. She could take a long weekend, or even a few days in the middle of the week without consulting anyone else's schedule. Granted, she didn't usually do that. But if the urge grabbed her, she certainly could.

Now, she had two unwanted, hell, unbelievable, guests in her house. Now, she was being told they were "stuck" in her world. She wasn't even sure she believed they were real. Yet, there they were.

"Isn't getting together with Kenn Cooper worth it, if it does nothing more than get us out of your life?" Blake asked, getting back to the point they unceremoniously dropped yesterday. "It's obvious you two were made for each other. Even in the all-too-short meeting you had."

"Please, aren't we getting ahead of ourselves?" She turned from the computer. It appeared getting any writing time in was going to be difficult. "And no, I cannot see how we were made for each other. I'd say we're more like polar opposites."

"Let's just stop for a moment and examine that phrase 'polar opposites'," he said. He rose from the loveseat and placed his index finger to his lips.

"Just what exactly does that mean? It could refer to the North and South Poles, in which case you and the professor have more in common than you think."

JJ and Alex looked at each other. "Is he always like this?"

Alex smiled. "You tell me. You created him."

"I'm having a problem dealing with this. Up until yesterday the two of you were only alive in my imagination. You weren't physically living in my office. No offense."

"None taken." The couple looked at each other to ensure they were in agreement on this one. Apparently, they were.

"But now, suddenly you literally pop up out of nowhere claiming to be characters from my book. You can see how this would skew a person's view of the world. Fictional characters are just that, fictional. They only reside in a person's mind. They just don't spring to life one day on a whim."

"Claim? Claim?" Blake took several steps toward JJ's desk. "You said we 'claim' to be characters from your book. You don't believe us?" He waved his arms, his hair dancing around his head. He certainly resembled the hero of her book, she thought, staring in amazement at the similarity.

"Who do you think we are if we aren't from your— I mean, our—love story? Where do you think we came from?"

She didn't need this. Hell, she hadn't even had her first cup of coffee yet. Surely even they had to admit this situation was at best a bit bizarre. At worst, it was totally unbelievable. How many more times did she have to try to process this?

They appeared frighteningly real. Perhaps she should visit a psychiatrist? She rubbed her temples.

"Coffee!" Blake suddenly and loudly announced as if it were the start of a race. "Coffee. That's what's missing from your morning. Let me make us, uhm, you, your morning coffee. You'll feel one-hundred percent better once you get that ole java flowing through your system. I know I'll feel better."

She waved her hand motioning him to go. He bounced out.

"I'm confused," she confessed as she looked at Alex, now on the loveseat. "If you two didn't leave, what did you do last night after I left?"

"Stayed in here, read some books, surfed the net, took turns sleeping on the loveseat."

She pursed her lips tightly. "I guess I just assumed that once I left, you would, well, go away. I assumed you were the result of my thoughts. Like a dream or a hallucination triggered by a lack of sleep and overwork. Either way, I just thought you'd go away."

"If it's any consolation," her heroine said, "I thought once you left the room, Blake and I would do just that— leave the room, too. I figured we'd just float back into our world again." She ran a hand through her hair. "I'm not sure how these things work. While coming to help you was a great idea, I guess it was one we didn't think through. And I didn't think returning to our world would be so difficult.

"And I know you have troubles of your own, with us just showing up uninvited, but I'm a little worried I may never get back to my world. I admit we really haven't investigated all avenues yet. But quite frankly, we made this journey on a whim. At some level I even doubted leaping into your world would work. But it did. And here we are."

She bit her lip and added, "I'm not sure about anything at the moment."

She gazed at the forlorn Alex. Yes, that's how she had envisioned her in one scene when Blake tells her they could never be together, that they weren't right for each other. It actually made her feel guilty for creating that emotion in her heroine.

"I hope you don't think I'm saying this because you literally gave me my world, but I really love it there. It's not that I don't love you, but…"

She fully believed Alex was about to cry. The scene really touched her.

"We'll get you back," she promised her. "There

25

must be a set of rules that could provide us with guidelines of what to do. In the meantime, we'll try to make you as comfortable and as at home here as we can. Okay?"

Alex shook her head meekly, like a little kid who had just been consoled over a loss of a toy by a parent.

"Coffee for all." Blake burst into the room, carrying a tray of three cups, milk, and sugar. His hair flipped outrageously from side to side as he jauntily stepped into the office. "I found some biscuits—oops, you guys call them cookies—for breakfast.

"But the food situation is looking a little pitiful down there, Ms. Spritely. I know you don't want to hear this, but we do need to eat. We may be fictional characters, but it appears we're equipped with some very real needs. And one of them is food."

JJ looked over at Alex who nodded her agreement. "I'm starved, personally."

"Okay, for starters, let me get dressed and then I'll run to the café to get a quick breakfast. With everything going on, I didn't realize how hungry I was too."

As she left the room, she said, "I won't be long. Later I'll go grocery shopping. As long as we're roommates, make yourself at home. The television's in the living room, find something good to watch, if you want."

She most assuredly didn't understand it, but for the moment, the couple seemed very real.

Chapter 7

"That's awfully nice of her," Blake said, shortly after JJ left. "I'm really not sure, love, how we're getting back. I'm a bit worried."

"I am, too, sweetheart. But what you said earlier, I think you're right. Our returning has something to do with JJ finding the love of her life. I've been thinking about it. I think we were sent on a mission." Alex's countenance brightened. "Once we fulfill that mission, we'll return to our own world."

He pursed his lips, as he thought about what she suggested.

Alex sighed. "Okay, so maybe it's not the most brilliant theory ever created."

"It's not a bad theory. You still have to fill a few gaping holes: Like who sent us here and who exactly is the love of JJ's life and how are we going to recognize him. Like this Kennedy Cooper person. How do we know that he's actually 'The One'?"

"Okay, I didn't say it was a perfect theory. But I don't see you creating a better plan. Any ideas, Einstein?"

"Not yet. But if we can't convince her that Kennedy Cooper is her true love, and the effort is not getting us very far yet, we may very well be here forever, according to your theory."

He took a gulp of coffee and tossed a cookie in his

mouth. "Oreos," he said, chewing enthusiastically, "my favorite."

She gazed at him a moment, lost in his eyes. The phone rang and startled her out of her romantic interlude. She looked at Blake who shook his head. "No," he added for emphasis.

"What could happen?" Not waiting for an answer, she grabbed the receiver. He grabbed the book he had been reading earlier.

She summoned her best professional voice. "Good morning, JJ Spritely's office, may I help you? No, I'm afraid she's not here at the moment, she's out running a few errands. May I take a message?"

"Well, just who am I speaking with?" She became defensive. "Oh, I'm sorry, Nan. JJ speaks of you often."

"Me? Who am I?" She flashed a panicked look over to Blake, but it was useless. He had buried himself in the book. JJ's history book to be exact, *The Historical Roots of Conspiracy Theories: America's Counter-History.* He seemed completely oblivious to the mess she found herself in. *How can he immerse himself in a book so quickly?*

Her immediate concern, though, was to answer Nan's pointed question.

"I'm...I'm...JJ's new personal administrative assistant. Yes, that's exactly who I am."

Apparently, this revelation proved awesome enough to bring Blake back from his historical journey. He peered quizzically out from behind the book. If she didn't know better, she would think he was laughing at her.

"When did she get an assistant?" Alex repeated Nan's question. "Uh, when did she hire me?

Hmm…gosh…how long…just last week. Yeah, yeah, just last week. I'm surprised your sister never mentioned it to you…"

Blake looked up from the book, knit his eyebrows in the what-are-you-talking-about look she could read so well.

"…considering," Alex continued, as she overacted and emphasized every word for Blake's benefit, "you and your sister are so close."

He started to chuckle and as his laughter increased, he sprinted out of the study, slamming the door behind him. She could still clearly hear him.

"Sure, Nan, I'd be happy to take a message. Dinner? Saturday night? Your place? There'll be you, your husband, Rob, JJ, and one other person."

Her face lit up. "You don't say? Oh, no, I don't know him. He's a history professor, you say? Well, well, what a coincidence."

If her mission in this world were to find the novelist a man—and not just any man, but a specific gentleman— then she just hit the jackpot.

"You know, Nan," she said, trying hard to show her excitement, "I'm looking over JJ's schedule now."

She stared at the blank computer screen. "She has nothing planned. Let me just pencil it in here and then if anything changes and she can't make it, she can call you."

She hung up the phone, and then gave serious thought of how she would get JJ to go to that dinner party. Obviously, the writer would resist if she had even an inkling of the other person on the guest list. She had to think of something before Saturday.

Chapter 8

JJ returned from her errand loaded with several bags. She found her characters in the living room. Blake apparently was testing out the cable.

Alex was sitting in the recliner on the other end of the room. "That's the plan," she said.

"What's the plan?" JJ said.

Her unexpected appearance startled Alex, who jumped out of the chair.

It was Blake, though, who acted the most suspicious.

"Well, it's nothing…n-n-nothing at all," he stammered, as he ran his fingers through his hair. His eyes darted toward his partner.

"Sounds suspiciously like something to me. I know you better than you think, so you better come clean. Am I in trouble? You have that look like you two were plotting something."

Alex quickly jumped in. "It's nothing we really wanted to bother you with, but do you think we could have a better place, well, actually some place to sleep tonight? It's not that I'm not grateful, but—"

"Sure. I'll get the second bedroom ready for you."

The three of them set up the TV trays and opened the Styrofoam food boxes as they talked.

"Your favorite brand of hot sauce is in the fridge," JJ said, not appearing to speak to anyone in particular.

Blake immediately jumped up and headed for the

refrigerator.

"I ordered your favorite breakfast," she continued as she turned to Alex. "French toast and two fluffy scrambled eggs with extra sharp cheddar cheese."

As an excited Blake entered the living room shaking the hot sauce, JJ said to him, "And you have nothing but your favorite, grape jelly."

"How'd you…?" Alex began, then laughed. "Is there anything you don't know about us?"

JJ stared into space for a moment as she thought about it. "Probably not."

"What if," Blake suggested, "our personalities begin to change ever so slightly while we're here? Would you know? And would you have control over it?"

JJ took a bite of her breakfast sandwich and raised her eyebrows. As she tilted her head, she answered, "I don't know. That's a good question. I've never been in this situation before. You two are the first to make the jump." *And with any luck, the last.*

"Listen to me, talking like this is normal. And then talking like I expect it to be one of multiple visits from my characters."

She paused. "Now I have a question for you. How did you know that I ran into that professor guy? What's his name?"

"Kennedy King Cooper," Blake answered. "There's an easy answer to that. You see, we are creations of your mind and that gives us certain privileges into your brain. Basically, as long as you're thinking about us in any way, we have access to just about all of your thoughts, and uhm…" She could see he was visibly uncomfortable continuing. "Well, Alex, you take it from here."

"And your emotional state at the time," she said

calmly.

"That's creepy," she admitted. "You two knowing just about everything about me."

"No creepier than you knowing all about us," Alex said.

"You've got a point there," she said as she took another bite of her breakfast sandwich.

"But I'm still lost how you got here. Did you follow a trail through the woods, did you jump into a black hole? Is there some type of portal between your world and mine?"

Blake drank some more coffee, placing his cup on the tray. "That puzzled me too," he said, suddenly sounding very serious. His usually light British accent grew more pronounced.

"It was an idea we came up with, talked about, and agreed on. And then before we realized it, our environment had changed. There seemed to be no rational explanation for it.

"But last night, when I couldn't sleep—"

"Sorry about that, guys," she apologized again.

He gave her the smile he usually reserved for Alex.

"I read some of the books in your library last night. I believe the explanation is easier than any of us ever imagined. In the volume you have, *The Essays of Ralph Waldo Emerson*, he states, that 'the ancestor of every action is a thought.'

"Smart man, especially for the time period he lived in. He was a student of—"

"Focus, honey. Focus," his partner encouraged. She put her fork down, placed her two hands about four inches apart from each other, as if she were creating some type of path, wagging her hands at him while urging him. "Stay. The. Course."

"Anyway, to become part of your book originally," he continued as if he didn't hear his love, "we had to have been a creation of your thoughts first. Now all this makes sense. What really intrigued me last night, though, was the comment by quite a few of the different writers that the universe cannot tell the difference between action based solely on thought, or imagination, if you will, and action based on hard core facts."

JJ stared at him, her home fries still on her fork.

"I don't get it," Alex admitted.

"Simple. Take the studies that were performed quite a while ago with basketball players," he explained. "The researchers told one group not to practice. Then they took a second group, instructing them to practice playing basketball in their minds. They were to imagine every detail they could, from the precise jump they used to dunking the ball, to the faces of the other players. 'Make it real,' they were told. And finally, they instructed the third group to physically practice thirty minutes a day." He paused, obviously for dramatic effect, JJ thought. "Do you know what happened?"

The two women stared at each other. Then they looked at him, shaking their heads. "What happened?" they asked in unison.

"The second group—who practiced in thought only—actually played a better game than the first group who did nothing."

Alex still shook her head. "What do basketball players have to do with us? I don't plan on playing basketball. Don't even try to get me on a court."

"The point goes deeper than basketball," Blake said patiently. "The concept holds that if you think about something long enough and believe hard enough that something—or in our case, two 'someones' are real—they become real."

She looked disappointed. "That's totally ridiculous."

JJ said nothing. She got up, gathered the paper her breakfast sandwich had been wrapped in, picked up her coffee cup, and headed for the kitchen.

"I'm going to work. If you guys need something let me know, I'll be in the office. Otherwise make yourselves at home."

Alex asked, "You'll be working all day, won't you?"

"That's the game plan. Except for the quick run to buy some groceries."

"Would you let us make you supper tonight? I'm sure between the two of us we can make something that's worth eating. It'll be our way of showing you we appreciate your hospitality."

JJ nodded and smiled. "Why thank you. How sweet." She strode into her office and closed the door.

What could possibly go wrong?

Chapter 9

"Fire! Fire!"

JJ heard Blake pummel on her office door. It sounded as if he were trying to break it down. "Save yourself first. No heroes, please! Women and children first!"

She jumped up in a panic and rushed to the door just as he pushed it open. She collided with him, and they both fell to their butts.

"Fire! Fire!" he continued to yell, trancelike.

"Okay! I get it!" She scrambled to her feet, leaving Blake struggling to stand. She practically trampled him in her beeline to the kitchen. She heard him get up and follow her.

Flames fanned out of the oven. "What's in there?"

"Pizza."

JJ opened the door beneath the sink, took the home fire extinguisher off the hook, and sprayed for the short period the device allowed. Thankfully, it was enough. The flames disappeared, and chemicals poisoned the air. She turned the oven off.

She grabbed a towel from a drawer under the counter and slowly approached the oven. She tentatively felt its handle. Cool enough to touch with the towel, she decided. She opened it.

It was hard to tell what was left of the pizza at first, but as she pulled it out, she realized it had been placed on the rack without being taken from the wrapper. Plastic had melted on the rack, the box, once green and red, was now curled and shades of burnt cardboard.

"What a bloody shame," Blake said. She shot him a dirty look.

She quickly surveyed the kitchen for the extent of the damage.

"Where's Alex?"

Blake's eyes widened. His mouth slowly formed an "O" formation, and he headed for the back door. He looked out past the small porch, over its wooden railing. She followed him.

There, not six feet from the porch, sat Alex. Her hair, which had been in a lightly pulled ponytail, was now strewn around her face which displayed a hurt and confused look. She stared up at the two of them as tears streamed down her cheeks.

"What happened?" JJ asked, as she pushed Blake aside to get to her.

"I was in the kitchen when he picked me up, carried me to the deck, and threw me over the railing."

****

"Who else wants a ham, pineapple, and ground beef slice of pizza?" Blake asked as he opened the pizza box on the coffee table. JJ looked at Alex, not knowing whether to laugh or to barf at the thought of the native Brit working on pizza slice number four.

"No, thank you, sweetheart. But I will take another of the chicken, onion, and green pepper, if you would please." She handed him her paper plate.

JJ looked at the two with a hint of satisfaction. There was some sort of pleasure knowing that these two individuals (could she call them that?) were of her very own creation. "How about you, JJ?" Alex asked. "Another piece of pizza?"

Not to be outdone, Blake offered his pineapple variety again. "I don't think I can handle pineapple and ground beef on a pizza together. But I'd love another piece of the chicken."

"Hurmph!" Blake tried to perform his best I'm-insulted routine. But it was no use. He couldn't keep it up very long. "You are a good sport for not giving me bloody hell for the kitchen," he said.

After the pizza boxes were packed away, the trio settled into the living room to watch some television.

"I know you guys didn't get much sleep last night," she said. "I just want you to know I fixed up the second bedroom for you. I won't be insulted if you want to turn in early."

They looked at each other. Even though it wasn't very late, the pair looked exhausted. Their trip through that imaginary portal couldn't have been easy, and then they got stuck in the small office last night. Yeah, everyone deserves a good night's sleep, she thought, even fictional characters.

They retired to the bedroom.

She wasn't ready to turn in, yet. She flipped through the television channels. Only now, with her characters out of sight, she gave her situation a little more thought. It seemed strange, but she had actually begun to accept that those two were real and they were, indeed, guests in her house for the moment.

If I don't accept this, what are the possible alternatives? Am I—?

Alex's shrill squealing abruptly brought the novelist back to the moment and on her feet.

"And don't come back."

Rushing to see what was wrong, she nearly collided with Blake, who was clad in only his boxer shorts, carrying a blanket and a pillow. Each of them screamed when they saw the other.

"What happened in there?"

"Apparently, we're not far enough along in our relationship to be in the same bed at the same time nearly naked. Mind if I use the loveseat in your office, again?"

"You can use the living room couch," she said as she sighed. "It's longer."

He held up the sleeping necessities in the international "would-you-look-at-this" fashion, as he took several calming breaths.

Then he softly said, "She let me have a pillow and blanket before she kicked me out." He paused. A smile crept over his face. "Evidently she does love me."

Chapter 10

The following morning JJ sat at her desk, took a deep breath, and began to write.

She furtively glanced his way, thinking he wasn't watching her. His dark, deep eyes quickly found hers. That stare penetrated her soul. In that moment, she knew what happened in the past didn't matter. The only thing that mattered was her realization she could live in this moment and love him with every fiber of her fabric. And she was willing to accept the consequences that went along with that serious decision.

She nodded her approval. In fact, no section of any of her books had ever made her so excited.

"This is a test," she muttered to herself. "This is only a test. Should this be a real-life romance situation, hero and heroine would be rushing toward each other in slow motion."

Would this get Alex and Blake together in the same bedroom at the same time so they could all finally get a decent night's sleep? We'd soon find out, she thought, as she hit the computer's save button.

Just then the office door flew open. Alex was breathless. And there was a glow about her.

"I got it. I got it," she shrieked over and over and again. "I've had a revelation. It just came to me. Out of the blue." She paused a beat.

"The past, the future doesn't matter. What matters is

right here, right now. And I don't want to pass up another moment with him. He's my sole reason for living."

She threw herself on the loveseat. JJ was worried. The experiment appeared to be exceeding her expectations.

Just then, Blake burst into the office.

"Aha!" he said, and in a twitch of an index finger he conveyed the power of his own personal revelation. The pair looked each other in the eyes as if playing a romantic game of dare. Neither lowered their gaze. Neither had to verbally express their thoughts.

The longer they held the stare, the more uncomfortable she felt. She wasn't accustomed to watching her scene unfold like a piece of theatrical drama.

"I think it's time for me to run some errands, I'll be back." She shut the computer down.

The pair failed to unlock their gaze. JJ added, "Maybe I'll grab a bite to eat, too. And, well, don't worry about me. I may be a while."

She picked up her messenger bag from beneath the desk that contained her laptop, plucked a book from the shelf, and began to ease out of the office.

"A long while." She scrambled out of the house as quickly as possible.

Chapter 11

Food and good coffee. That's what every decent romance writer wants after writing the ultimate love scene (well, maybe a little bit more, but food and good coffee would do). In the town of Bell Wyck, Ohio, that only meant one place: the Physics Café. The city's most popular casual dining establishment, the Physics Café was a special favorite of the students, faculty, and staff of the University of Northern Ohio.

She opened the door to the café, and the buzz of customers' conversations and laughter hit her. Busier than I expected, JJ thought. She scanned the walls as she strode toward the front. The photos of the physicists that hung on the wall above the booths and tables reminded her of her first visit. She had gone in on a lark, intrigued by the name. She recalled not recognizing any of the scientists except for Einstein. Today, she nodded to Marie Curie, Erwin Schrodinger, Max Planck, and others.

Indeed, she even could tell you what the mathematical equations were that accompanied many of the photos. She felt smarter just walking in.

Three physics geeks (that was the only way to describe them) opened the café several years ago, mostly on a dare. They complained one day, so the story goes, they were tired of glamorous themed restaurants. Anyone could make money in a restaurant like *Hard*

Rock Café. But it would take a bit of business acumen, they said, to make money from an eatery where the glamorous celebrities were all physicists, like Einstein, Max Planck, and Niels Bohr.

They claimed they could open a restaurant aimed at the "geek" market and make a killing. A group of businessmen overheard their conversation, challenged them, and even offered to back them financially. And the Physics Café was born.

She was pleased to see Alvin working the register. He, along with Simon and Ted, were the three geeks. And he looked every bit the part. He was tall and lanky, with short, brown hair. His green eyes were hidden behind large, round, black glasses.

"It's been a while, doctor," Alvin said as he flashed a smile and nudged his glasses up the bridge of his nose.

"It's been too long," she answered. "You're busier than I remembered."

"Our lunch crowd," Alvin explained. "It seems to start earlier with every passing week." He paused as if he were unsure of what to say next. "What can I get you?"

She picked up a menu on the counter and instantly found what she wanted. The Philadelphia Experiment Cheesesteak. As the menu described it, the sandwich was "a classic Philly cheesesteak with a twist. The sautéed onions on this sandwich are treated by our very own de-particlizer. While your sandwich appears to have onions, should they disappear while you're eating your meal, you'll receive a free cappuccino."

"I'd like a side of Onion String Theory with that too," she said. A White Chocolate Dark Matter Cappuccino completed her order.

"What size?" Alvin asked, "Dwarf, nova, or super

nova?"

"Dwarf," she answered. She paid for her meal and Alvin handed her the placard with her order number on it. "We'll call your number as soon as we can, doctor." She saw it was 26Fe, the periodic number for the element iron.

"And this is just one more reason I love this place."

She went in search of a seat. All four booths along the left side of the café were taken. The tables in the front of the coffee shop were filled with students, staring at their laptops, every so often nudging their neighbor to look at their screen, or engaged in animated conversation.

Frustrated with the lack of available tables, she finally found an empty spot at the laptop counter. It wasn't the most glamorous seat nor the most comfortable, but the counter, built against a four-foot free-standing wall, provided plenty of electrical outlets.

She carefully eased herself between two male customers, both of whom appeared to be concentrating on an internet search. She imagined they were in a search of life's most difficult questions no doubt: what celebrity made an ass of himself today?

While she waited for her order, she opened the book she had brought along. An alternative view of President Warren G. Harding's death, it claimed that Harding's wife actually poisoned him. She had been meaning to read it for what seemed like forever. Maybe I have been writing too much, she thought with shrug.

She took a five-by-seven inch spiral notebook and a pen out of her bag and laid them next to the book. It has been far too long, she thought, that I actually did historical research. And what better book to re-ignite my interest? Maybe someday I'll write another history book. Just the thought of it made her happy. She had missed history and teaching, she realized, more than she had imagined.

As she was just settling in, she heard her element called. She tried to get up as gently as possible without disturbing the two persons between her. She retrieved her food and once again faced the tricky problem of getting back into the tight quarters.

In the process, though, she bumped the gentleman to her right. "Excuse me," she automatically said. That's when she really looked at him. And almost screamed in revulsion. Please, she pleaded to the forces in the universe responsible for the galactic seating arrangement, this can't be happening to me. Not here. Not now. But it was. It was him—with a capital "H." Kennedy King Cooper. Again.

Their eyes locked. A cold shiver seared down her spine. Not again. It was evident he recognized her. But would he say anything? And did she really want to talk to him?

She forced a smile and quickly stuck her head back in the book. But it was too late. Her body was beginning to go limp with uninvited sexual attraction. Damn that love scene. She had discovered that this reaction to good-looking men was an occupational hazard for romance writers.

Could it really be that her fictional friends saw something she was too blind to see? She pushed that idea from her head. That was just stupid.

Suddenly, she could hear his words. Calm yourself, she told herself. Just calm yourself. Good looking. Check. Sexual attraction. Check. Can you build a lasting relationship on that alone? Of course not. Would she like to give it a try? Check. No. What was she thinking? No. She reminded herself of his attitude toward romance writers. That helped. A little.

"I see you got the Philly Experiment," Kenn said. She nodded. She didn't trust her voice to speak to him. Why? Was she afraid she'd act on her urges? Nonsense.

"And the onions are there." She mustered up the courage to say something. "No free cappuccino for me."

"Maybe next time. There's always that off-chance their de-particlizer will work."

"I'm not holding my breath on that one." She took a bite of the sandwich and forced herself to read. She feared if she kept talking, she would commit herself to some type of date that she wouldn't ordinarily agree to. She believed she was still "under the influence" of romance novelist's idealism. Nothing more.

Just as she was getting highlighting pens out and sticky notes for page references, Cooper continued the conversation. *Damn him*. He questioned her about the book she was reading.

"That book looks interesting. I never dealt much with Harding, but I find him and his Teapot Dome scandal pretty fascinating." She didn't dare tell him what she was really researching. He would undoubtedly have the same response many of her colleagues had when you mention the word conspiracy.

"You know, there's a conspiracy theory floating around the internet that Harding didn't die of accidental food poisoning," Kenn began.

"Many believe," JJ continued, "that his wife actually poisoned him."

"You've heard it, too? That's absolutely absurd."

Why do some men have to be so smug in their opinions? They voice an opinion as if it's fact. She just shook her head, while she decided how to respond.

She worked extra hard at maintaining an outward composure. But inwardly she was furious. Who was he after all to declare it absurd?

Instead of lashing out in anger, she merely smiled, commenting, "Hell hath no fury like a woman scorned. And Mrs. Harding, from what I've read, felt scorned. After all, it was rumored Harding was quite the womanizer."

"But would she really kill her husband over these actions?"

"Let me play devil's advocate a moment," she suggested. Kenn nodded in agreement. "Let's say she didn't kill him because of that, but because she was fearful he would soon be implicated in the web of corruption that was surrounding his administration. Is that a motive for murder?"

He placed the Chernobyl Chicken Meltdown he had been holding on his plate. "Would his wife kill him basically to save his reputation? Doesn't seem like a good trade-off to me. No, no. I can't buy that one. I think only a lazy historian would accept that conspiracy theory."

"Lazy?" Impetuously, she leapt from her seat. *Thud.* Her chair fell backward in the process, causing a number of customers to stare. She stomped around it as best she could in such tight quarters. She started to raise the chair at the same time Kenn bent over to help pull it upright. Their hands touched. The rage that had circulated through her felt more like passion now.

Hurriedly, she gathered her things and looked Kenn

square in the eyes. He possessed the kindest, most compassionate eyes she had ever seen. Her rage melting, she began to feel…was that vulnerable? Still, his remark was careless and judgmental.

"Listen, just because a historian wants to explore an unconventional topic does not make him or her lazy." She could feel the tension in her jaw build as she tried to keep her voice down, her words measured. "Every good historian needs to be open minded to all the possibilities."

Her appetite was lost. She hurriedly gathered her book, notebook, and pens and shoved them in the messenger bag. And she left without saying another word, leaving her sandwich and onion strings behind.

Chapter 12

Alex lingered in bed, her head resting in the crook of Blake's arm. "It was magical," she whispered. "You are magic."

He pulled her even closer. "It was, love. I can't imagine—"

Blake never got the chance to finish his thought.

"If anyone had any lingering doubts," JJ announced as she entered the house, "like you Alex, wherever you are, you can just wipe them from your mind."

Alex shot up and hastily pulled on some type of covering. Blake reached for the nearest thing to cover him. Alex, wrapped in a robe and Blake, shrouded in a blanket, timidly stepped out the bedroom door. Alex was the first to speak. "You ran into him again?"

"Yes, I did. And I can confirm unequivocally that man is one humongous pompous ass." JJ threw her purse across the living room to the far side of the couch.

She looked at the pair, her eyes opening wide, her mouth involuntarily forming a smile. "What?" Blake questioned.

"It's just awkward for me, that's all. It's like a bad horror movie."

Chapter 13

"You what?" Without waiting for a response, JJ continued. "How could you possibly confirm a dinner date for me without even leaving a note somewhere?"

"I'm sorry, JJ. It just slipped my mind." It was Saturday afternoon, and the truth was Alex could think of nothing else for the last couple of days. The prospect of JJ seeing this man again filled her thoughts, and very romantic ones they were.

Several different factors motivated her. Well, of course, she wanted for JJ what her creator had given her: a gorgeous man who loved her. She already recognized that JJ used her work as a thinly veiled attempt to hide her loneliness.

But she also wanted to get back to her own world, her own life, the tending to her small flower garden, to her cat, Mr. Whiskers, and the very personal unfolding of her life with Blake. She was eager to see where it all was going to lead.

She prayed that JJ would feel the social pressure to go to her sister's. So far, the plan was going just as she had envisioned. Anger. She knew JJ would be furious when she learned of the dinner party. She had expected that and accepted it. Now, she crossed her fingers JJ would do exactly what she had expected of her—go anyway. It really was too late to call and back out.

Alex was more than willing to bear both the brunt of

the anger and the criticism if it meant getting JJ to her sister's. This would result in her encountering Professor Cooper again. More importantly, if all went well, it would result in her falling in love with him.

As these thoughts filled her mind, she heard the continuing rant, "Do you have any idea how much I'd love to call right now and tell Nan I'm not coming? But it's a little late. I'm supposed to be there in three hours."

JJ, who had been leisurely curled up on the living room couch, remote control in one hand while the other had been digging through the popcorn bowl, brought her feet from the couch to the floor, in an exaggerated, agitated manner. Sighing deeply, she glared at Alex, who in turn, looked down at her shoes, as she attempted to put a remorseful look on her face.

She knew this event meant nothing less than JJ fulfilling her destiny. Destiny. Synchronicity. The magical alignment of the stars. Kismet. Whatever you want to call this moment, she thought romantically, it appeared the Universe was working toward finding a soul mate for the very person who brought her own soul mate into her life.

The one thing she didn't want was to screw this up. It was best, as far as the "flow of the Universe" was concerned, that JJ be carried along by the tide of events—even if it meant blindfolding her to those events and dragging her along kicking and screaming.

JJ finally paused in her tirade and rose from her place on the couch. Alex quickly and quietly stepped in to speak. "I suppose if you're going, you should start to get ready."

JJ glowered fiercely at her. "You have no right meddling in my personal life. How dare you make a…"

JJ began to say something more then stopped. A strange look came over her face. "Let me get this straight," she said, a little softer and in a more thoughtful manner. "You talked to my sister over the telephone?"

"Yeah, sure." Alex paused.

"And she heard you and spoke to you?"

"That's usually how those conversations work." Alex bit her lip.

Blake, who had been sitting on the wingback chair, put his book down. "What's your point?"

Ah, Blake would get to the bottom of this for her. Thank you, hon, she said to herself.

"My point is that a phone conversation has to take place between two real people." JJ paced the small living room as she spoke. "Up until now, I just assumed I was the only person who could interact with you two. That you were figments of my imagination."

"No," Alex whimpered. "That's so mean." Blake leaped out of the chair and wrapped an arm around Alex.

"This changes everything." JJ sat on the edge of the couch.

Alex, who was still in the protective hold of Blake, tilted her head. "How so?"

"Don't you see, love?" Blake's answer not only startled Alex but JJ as well.

"No, I don't. Someone please explain it to me. All I did was talk to JJ's sister."

"If we were solely a part of your imagination," Blake said, addressing JJ, "then Alex wouldn't have been able to talk to your sister, right?"

JJ nodded. "Exactly. If no one else can talk to you, then I can be pretty comfortable that I'm the one going through this, well, whatever it is. But, if everyone can talk to you and see you, then I'm not entirely sure what's going on here. Up until now, you were my personal, private hallucinations. I'm just not sure what to call you now."

"Try calling us real," Alex said, one hand on her hip.

"But real is impossible. It defies all the currently known scientific laws. What if everyone could see you, not just me, as I just naturally assumed so far?"

Alex sat on the arm of the couch, near JJ. "I'm still confused. I don't get what the big deal is."

Blake paced the room, his head down, hands behind his back. "Aside from your conversation with JJ's sister, love, we haven't had an occasion to have contact with anyone."

"Right," JJ agreed. "I assumed you couldn't interact with others. Now, I wonder if others could see you, too." She rubbed the back of her neck.

Blake rose and padded to the front door. Alex watched as he unlocked and opened the door. Then he turned. "Alex, let's test out my theory."

"Me? What are we going to do?"

"You'll see."

Alex shot a quick glance at JJ, who only looked amused by her perplexity. She figured she had little choice and met Blake at the door. He took her hand and they stepped on onto the small porch. She scanned the neighborhood. Everyone had at least a little patch of yard.

One house sported the stereotypical white picket fence. The house directly to the right wore a shiny metal flowerpot of purple petunias, yellow and purple pansies, and a few tall dark pink snapdragons. A few houses down she saw that one house had a wraparound porch with baskets of red geraniums adorning it.

Finally, she saw an older gentleman who lived directly across the street. He was out with his golden Labrador retriever.

"Good afternoon," Blake called out to him, waving as if he were the proverbial friendly neighbor.

"I'm Bob Higley, and this is Moses." The man gave the dog a good rub.

"I'm Blake Teesdale and my fiancé, Alex Zurich. She's JJ's cousin from Kansas and we're here on vacation." Alex smiled meekly and gave the man a tentative finger wave. She was amazed at his ability to create an entire backstory on the spot.

Mr. Higley took off his baseball cap and scratched his head. "You don't sound like you're from Kansas."

"No, no sir. You are right. Mine is definitely not a Midwest accent. British."

"I've always loved England."

"Thanks, I love your country too." And then Blake gave Mr. Higley a friendly good-bye wave and he and Alex went back into the house.

Once inside, he rolled on the balls of his feet, a small, smug smile slowly forming on his lips, hands in his pockets.

"We just passed the can-they-see-you test with flying colors. And yes, they can see you—I mean, us."

"Yes, you two did and I'm amazed."

Alex looked at the living room clock. "JJ, I don't mean to bring up a sore subject, but it is getting closer to the time."

"Yes, it is now, isn't it?" She glowered again at Alex. "We're not completely done with this topic. You and I are going to sit down and talk, soon."

Chapter 14

JJ marched out of the living room. Despite the remarkable experiment of Blake's, she was still peeved at the fact that she had to go to this dinner party. As she got into the shower, she tried to put the events of the last several days out of her mind.

She allowed the hot water to beat down on her, to run down her back, to massage her tired, sore shoulders, to gently lift the stresses of the day from them. Having visitors took its toll on her.

Well, that wasn't quite right. Not knowing how they got there or if she was just going crazy was the real stressor. The next thing she knew she had tears running down her face.

Tears. Yes, she was tired of dealing with just about everything. The unplanned visit of Alex and Blake shook her to her core. She didn't want to go to her sister's and play social butterfly.

As much as she loved Nan, she would have preferred to spend the Saturday evening at home alone—okay, almost alone. But definitely on her own couch, in her own cocoon of her home, curled up with some book that took her thoughts off of what her life was like right now.

The tears that fell freely in the shower had more to do with her frustration at being in a place in her life she really didn't want and hadn't planned on—at least not at such a young age. "My friends still have their parents around," she thought, "and here at twenty-eight, not only are my parents gone, I don't even have my husband."

She realized in these moments when she let her guard down how much she missed Geoff. Witnessing just how solicitous Blake was to Alex, the obvious love the two had for each other and the tender (and now passionate) way they looked at one another, aroused feelings she had tried hard to keep buried.

She recalled seeing them exit the bedroom half-clothed the other day. She felt not so much an awkwardness but a small bite of envy. *Would I ever know those feelings again? Or was I destined only to write about them in my books?*

God, these were questions she preferred not to ask. Emotions she preferred not to acknowledge, let alone deal with. She had submerged them, the loneliness, the grief, the longing to be loved by a man.

She had hoped they would simply disappear. But they hadn't. They had only grown fiercer and would occasionally—like right now—explode unexpectedly to the surface of that sea of emotional turmoil, threatening the core of her daily living.

Of course, there was a reason why she hid them so well. If she actually dealt with them, she was afraid she would begin to question absolutely everything that was left of her life. And quite frankly, there wasn't much.

Except her writing. She clung to her writing like the passengers of the Titanic had clung to their life rafts and shards of the ship. She saw her life as the Titanic, and she was drowning fast in icy cold water.

Chapter 15

Kenn Cooper had just settled into his recliner with a beer, clicked on the sports channel, and was prepared to have a perfectly lazy Saturday afternoon. The fall term would begin soon and any hope of another day like this was far in the future.

Then the phone rang. "I sure hope this isn't my mother." He picked up the phone and looked at the caller ID before answering. He figured he could let it go to voice mail if it was his mom.

The number wasn't his mom's but Deb Dilley's. "Why would she call me at home? Don't tell me Dr. Chare needs something." He let it ring two more times as he considered whether to answer. His conscience got the better of him.

"Deb, what's so important you had to call me at home?"

"You what?" He bounded out of the recliner, clenching the phone. "Did you just say you accepted a dinner invitation on my behalf?" He took a deep breath. "And just now telling me about it?"

"Yes, sir." Deb's whispered response was barely audible.

"How could you? Deb, I swear..." He had no words. His plans of doing absolutely nothing had just imploded. The audacity of that woman.

"I'm sorry, Dr. Cooper, it slipped my mind."

"How in the hell can something like that slip your mind?" He took a deep breath, as he tried to make sense out of the insane situation.

"I don't know what you're doing even accepting social appointments on my behalf. You're the history department secretary, not my personal one." He ran a hand through his hair.

How dare Deb call him at home—on a Saturday no less—and tell him he had to be at Rob's—he looked at his watch—in less than two hours. Holy crap!

"You could have left me a note, you know?"

"Yes, I suppose I could have."

A dinner party at Rob's. Even though Deb didn't mention it, he knew there would be a fourth person at the dinner table. Some woman Rob, or more precisely his wife, had handpicked for him. It was her not-so-subtle way of playing matchmaker. Didn't he and Rob just have this conversation? Didn't he say he wasn't interested?

His experience told him it would end less than successfully. And right now, he certainly wasn't interested in being set up with some strange woman. Then he remembered he still had Deb on the phone.

"Deb, this is a serious transgression. You know darn well it's too late for me to cancel, even though I want to. I'll deal with you Monday. In the meantime, I need to get ready." He clicked his phone off, not caring to even end the call politely.

He sat for a moment. While he normally disliked Rob trying to set him up, this instance was particularly repugnant. Honestly, he admitted to himself, the only woman he wanted to see was the one he met at the bookstore. *I can guarantee she's not going to be there.*

He wasn't sure what word described his longing to

see her again. Was it curiosity? Infatuation? Obsession? The truth was in the short couple days since he met her, he thought about her more than he cared to admit.

He pushed all of that out of his mind and mentally braced himself for what awaited him.

****

When Kenn arrived at Rob's, he was relieved to discover there were no other guests. He took a seat in the same wingback chair he always sat in for his visits. Rob and Nan sat on the couch. "Glad you could make it," Rob said.

He laughed, explained how he didn't get the message until just a few hours ago. "Frankly, I thought you were trying to set me up with someone again. I'm glad to see it's just the three of us."

Nan coughed and nudged Rob in the ribs. "Well, to be honest, there is one more person coming."

He let out a sigh. "I'm not interested in dating anyone right now." He shifted his weight in the chair.

"We know you aren't, Kenn," Rob said. "That's not what this evening's about. We invited Nan's sister. We have her over quite a bit, but she really needs to talk to people other than us." He glanced at Nan. "She's a widow and has been burying herself in her work. We're trying to get her out of the house more, that's all." He paused. "She's also a history buff. We thought she'd enjoy meeting and talking with you."

Every muscle in his body relaxed. "I can't tell how relieved I am to hear that." He envisioned an older woman, white hair, on the plump side. Just then the doorbell rang.

Chapter 16

JJ pulled her car up the driveway of her sister's Cape Cod. She admired the large maple tree in the front yard and how the late afternoon sun highlighted the leaves just beginning to turn colors.

The house, painted a snappy white with a crisp crimson trim, had an attached garage Rob had added several years ago. A large, red metal star hung over its door.

She exited the car and walked up to the front porch, furnished with four wicker chairs and two small end tables. She stood at the door and took a deep breath. To say she wasn't looking forward to this was the understatement of the century. But she was determined to be polite for Nan's sake. And, should her determination fail her, the bottle of wine she brought as a hostess gift would strengthen her resolve. She hoped.

This was not the first round of draft choices for her new husband. While she continually protested these dinners, her sister cheerfully and deliberately continued holding them. She knew her sister meant well.

She explained several times over to her sister she had a different set of priorities now. When the time came, she knew the right man would walk into her life. Until then, men were just not a major attraction. Or so she tried to convince herself.

Her mind went over the obstacles to dating. It had

only been four years. Far too early to be seeing anyone yet, let alone thinking about a serious relationship. And she couldn't even imagine replacing the image of Geoff with some other man. It was just totally impossible. So, what were all those sensual feelings she had at the café the other day for Kenn Cooper?

Enough. She purposely pushed such thoughts from her head. She refocused on where she was, feeling like a Christian about to enter the lion's den. She rang the doorbell, and without waiting for an answer, let herself in.

As she walked into her sister's living room, she pasted an automatic smile on her face. It wasn't difficult; she loved her sister. Nan brought out the best in her. Nan jumped off the couch and the two sisters hugged. JJ handed her the bottle of wine.

Rob and the guest stood up. As the siblings released their embrace, Rob stepped up to give her sister-in-law a kiss on the cheek.

"I'd like you to meet…"

"You!" Every muscle in her body tightened.

"Dr. Kennedy King Cooper," Rob whimpered.

Making no pretense of even being polite to Kenn, she quickly, and awkwardly dragged her sister by the arm out of the room. Nan's free arm flailing, she managed a smile and a single index finger wave to the men.

"Back in a nanosecond," she said with what sounded like more than a bit of uncertainty.

As they left the room, she heard Rob say, "Well, I'd say that went rather well, now, didn't it?"

"Nan, how in the world could you do this me?" she asked when they reached the kitchen. Absolutely infuriated with her sister, she paced frantically.

"After I told you I didn't want you to try to set me up with any guy, you set me up with the man I met in the bookstore. He's a complete egotistical maniac."

"Honey, you knew who were meeting tonight. You should have said something."

She gave her sister a blank stare.

"I told your personal assistant the guest was a friend of Rob's from your old history department. I even mentioned his name—I'm sure I did. She assured me she'd give you all the details."

"Is that what she called herself when she answered the phone—my personal assistant?"

"Well, if she's not that, who is she?"

"Alex. Alex Zurich, she's one of the characters…" she almost said it. *One of the characters from my novel.*

"You're right, she's my new personal assistant." She sighed and rolled her eyes.

"I didn't mention it to you because I wasn't sure if you'd see hiring her as an extravagance or not." She examined her horrible circumstances—from the vain man in the living room who made her livid just thinking about him to the two characters from her novel in her own living room.

"Come on, give the man a break," Nan urged. "Maybe he's not as bad as you think. After all, he was Rob's roommate in college. Rob's got pretty good taste. He married me, didn't he?"

"Yeah, and that's probably the last smart decision about people he's made. In the last three months he's dragged home a boring accountant, a less-than-mesmerizing electrical engineer, and a computer programmer whose sole hobby is playing video games.

All in the hopes of trying to find me a husband."

Before Nan could respond, she continued, "Now, I'm sure they're all fine men, but I had absolutely nothing in common with them. Come to think of it, Rob and that computer programmer had a great time together after supper playing video games."

"Yes, that was less than successful, I admit that. But Rob has learned from his mistakes. That's why he thought you and Kenn would have something in common. You're both history nuts."

"And of all the 'history nuts' in the world, who would think that Rob would choose the one who hates romance writers like me? Which, by the way, is my new career."

"I don't think Rob got far enough in the conversation to explain that you're now a full-time romance novelist. And I'm positive he didn't know this was the guy you met at the bookstore."

"Did Cooper know when he accepted the invitation I was going to be the woman Rob wanted him to meet? Because had you mentioned my name—or even that I'm now 'officially' retired from academic life and writing romances, he never would have accepted. I'm sure of it. I'm telling you, our little encounter was less than pleasant."

"I heard Rob tell someone on the phone, but he told me he left a message with the secretary."

"That sounds familiar," she muttered, thinking back to how she got corralled into coming. "I assume the secretary is still Debra Dilley. And I can just imagine what she said. 'I'll have Kenn call you if there's a problem with this.'"

Nan looked amazed. "Well, yeah. I think that's

exactly what she told him, but how did you know?"

"Remember? I used to work there. And I know Deb." She shook her head. "If he would have known there was some romance author here, even if he didn't remember my name, he never would have accepted the invitation, either. His dislike for creatures"—she flashed air quotes—"like me is that great."

"Oh, stop being so melodramatic. This isn't one of your novels. Maybe you just misread him. He seems like a very nice man. Besides, can't you put your romance writer hat aside for just one evening to meet him on some common ground?"

Typically, a remark like that would not have even bothered her, but the pressures of the last several days were bearing down on the normally impish writer.

"No. I cannot. And what are you implying? That you're ashamed of my new profession? You want me to hide it?"

"No, not at all, but couldn't you just—?"

"Just what?" JJ cut her off. She grabbed her sister's hand and began pulling her. She headed for the bedroom.

Along the way, they passed the living room, where the men were apparently engaged in a similar conversation. "Excuse us one moment, gentlemen, Nan has something to show me, don't you, Nan?" JJ said as she dragged her sister past them. Her sister, a hopeless look plastered on her face, nodded slowly, and shrugged.

When they reached the master bedroom, she shut the door and locked it.

"What are you doing? Have you gone mad?" Nan asked.

"No, I just happen to know that at the far end of your walk-in closet," she began as she switched the closet light on, "you have a bookcase." She pulled her sister over to it. "And oh, by the way, it's filled with nothing but—oh, look—romance novels. And oh, look. Upon closer inspection, not one of them is mine. So, you can't say that you're just collecting my novels. You are a closet romance novel reader."

At the realization of the horrible pun, the sisters burst out laughing.

****

Finally, the four of them were in the same room at the same time. JJ reluctantly sat next to Kenn at the small round table. Then realizing how close they were sitting, she stood up, walked behind the chair, and moved it about six inches away from him and closer to Nan. She pushed and shoved her legs between her sister's chair and her own as she sat back down. Satisfied with the space separating them, she took a healthy drink of the red wine already poured. Rob and Kenn shared a confused look as they watched this elaborate performance.

Unfortunately, she still felt some of the sexual chemistry she experienced at the Physics Café. Those "love-scene residuals," as she called them, flared up again. And there was that scent of his cologne again, darn it. Boy, it was distinctive. And boy, did it drive her crazy.

As Nan passed the main course of roast beef around, she nervously made small talk.

"Kenn, did you know that JJ used to be on the history faculty of the University of Northern Ohio?"

Kenn shook his head. "I knew she had been a history professor. I didn't realize it was at UNO."

"Yeah, she wrote the book," Rob said, *"The Historical—"*

"That's all history now, as they say," JJ interrupted,

64

as she waved the biscuit she just plucked from the basket being passed around.

"Here, Kenn, have a biscuit." She shoved the basket of biscuits into his hand.

She already knew his views on conspiracy theories. *Let's not bring that up again. Good grief, the publication of the book caused enough controversy originally. No need to replay the same scenes.*

The general public loved *The Historical Roots of Conspiracy Theories: America's Counter History.* It was the first time many of the theories had been seriously examined by a professional historian. The academic community, however, was divided in their opinions. Some commended the topic and the quality of research. Others saw it as a black smudge on the field.

"I'm a full-time romance author now, but I think you already know that." She gave him the sweetest smile she could muster. And that was it. She vowed she wasn't going to speak a word about her novels or about the subject of her nonfiction book.

But Kenn evidently had other plans and plowed on with the topic.

"Why would women even bother reading fluffy novels like that?" The tone of the question seemed sincere, but it must have struck a chord with Rob, who was pouring gravy on his meal. He dropped the gravy boat, splashing hot gravy over himself and his wife.

He hurriedly tried to clean himself up as he and Nan left from the room. JJ and Kenn, however, were only getting started on their literary discussion and didn't even notice it.

"Why would anyone want to shut their brain down like that?"

She slung the biscuit she had in her hand on her plate. It bounced into the middle of the table.

"Because in a romance novel not one person worries about how they're going to pay the cable bill this month. Not one person winces when the price of milk creeps up another couple of cents."

As she talked, she saw how Kenn looked at her. His gaze appeared more than just cursory. His eyes were riveted on hers—not on any other part of her or anywhere else in the room. It was as if he listened with his eyes.

As she explained the attraction of romance novels, she knew she had his full attention. She wanted him to feel the full force of her anger, but she discovered his gaze calmed her.

"I'm glad we men don't have to read stuff like that to feel better about our lives."

That was all it took. She suddenly forgot about Kenn's incredibly kind eyes, the sensual attraction that she felt when near him, the scent of his cologne. Once again, he implied that men were somehow superior based on his independently derived idea that romance as a story was trash.

"Oh, and you don't think you guys have your own version of feel-good books and movies out there. You men have a category of movie that's the equivalent of our romance novel—it's called the action movie." She waved a hand as if she were demonstrating the wealth of the genre.

"Pick your favorite action hero or your favorite cowboy. The movies these heroes star in are nothing more than flights of fantasy for the testosterone set."

Chapter 17

"I can just imagine the wonderful, romantic time JJ is having at this very moment." Alex sighed. Curled up in the crook of Blake's shoulder as she stared off into space for a moment. With their first evening without JJ, the two were on the couch watching a movie.

"You do realize two other people are present at this romantic dinner," Blake said, as he kissed her on the top of her head. "I'm not sure how romantic that is."

"When two people are in love, no one else is in the room. They see only each other." Alex looked into her love's eyes. "Besides, the sooner they discover each other, the sooner we can go home."

But it didn't appear that he was listening. "Wait, I want to see what happens next," he said, as he pointed at the television screen. "The good witch is telling Dorothy how to get home."

They watched in silence.

"Yeah, so?" She didn't see any significance in the scene.

"If she can use that mode of transportation to get to another world, so can we," he said. "Maybe it's a Universal law we've overlooked.

"Oh. My. Heavens. Of course, we've had the power all along to go home, too."

She jumped up and pulled Blake with her. "Let's do it right now."

"Not yet. I think to replicate this event properly, we should recreate every facet of it as closely as possible."

She knitted her brow, then a smile flashed across her face. "Let's dig through JJ's closet." And she dragged him into JJ's bedroom.

****

Alex heard the shower running. Then it stopped. "We're off to see the…" Blake's singing grated through the air, like fingernails on a chalkboard.

She was already dressed, and in place. And impatient. Finally, he emerged from the bathroom with only a towel around him. His head bobbed as he skipped down the hall, his wet hair splashing drops of water like a dog shaking his whole body when it's wet.

"What is taking so long?" she asked.

"It takes time for me to beautify, baby."

She closed her eyes and shook her head. He continued his skipping and headed for JJ's bedroom.

"I'll be all dressed in just a second, love," he called as he closed the door.

While she waited for him to emerge from the bedroom, she alternatively paced, adjusted her—well, actually JJ's—white dress, and nervously ran her fingers through her hair.

She finally sat on the couch a moment, quickly removed the red pumps, and rubbed her feet. JJ's feet were several sizes smaller than hers. Then, she thought of poor Blake. He had even larger feet. *How would he…?* She was putting her shoes back on when she heard the bedroom door open.

"Oh, Alex," he chimed. "I'm ready. And I'm coming out."

And with that Alex heard the clicks of the heels on

68

the hardwood hallway. "Damn it!" *Click.* "Bloody heels." *Click.* "How do you women wear these things?" *Click.* "Oh, my aching back!"

His voice grew louder till he reached the living room where she was standing expectantly. She couldn't believe what she saw. Standing in front of her was the man she loved, dressed nearly exactly as she was. The white dress was barely long enough to cover even a small fraction of his thighs his feet were stuffed into a pair of red stiletto heels

"Love," he said grimacing through his pain, "does this outfit make me look fat?"

She merely shook her head. Then she noticed something even more bizarre about him.

"Are those pantyhose you're wearing?"

"Yeah, but they barely come to my waist. I never realized how short JJ was till I put on her pantyhose."

She doubled over in laughter. He appeared so sincere yet looked so ridiculous. "Uhm, dear, do you know how short that dress is on you?"

"Hey, it's not my fault. It's not like I was shopping at Harrods. JJ had two white dresses in her closet, and you picked the better of the two. My choices were limited."

He turned his back to her. "Look, I can't even button this bloody thing." At the sight of the open white dress against his hairy back, she laughed uncontrollably.

"What's so funny?" he asked, as he planted his hands on his hips. "You get to wear the good Dorothy dress. I'm stuck with this." He looked down at his apparel.

"I just want to make sure we have every detail in place, just in case it's not the ruby slippers that actually work the magic." He took a deep breath and held out his hand.

"Now could we get on with this please? I think these pantyhose are strangling my manhood."

They held hands, closed their eyes and clicked their heels together. Secretly, Alex prayed the red-heeled shoes would be a good enough substitute for the ruby slippers.

"Okay, at the count of three," Blake instructed. Alex nodded. "One, two, three. There's no place like home. There's no place like home. There's no place like home." When they opened their eyes, they were still standing in JJ's living room.

"Let's try it one more time," Blake urged, "just in case the Universe was busy doing something else and wasn't listening." Disappointed and on the verge of tears, she slowly nodded her assent.

They had resumed their stance and held hands when she heard JJ walk in through the back door. As the writer entered the living room, she asked, "What in the world is going on? Blake, is that you in that dress?"

The sharpness of JJ's voice sparked the flood of tears Alex had tried to hold back. She was so frustrated. She only wanted to return to her world, check on her cat, and make sure that pot of soup she had started hadn't boiled over. She didn't believe JJ when she said she took care of it for her.

Blake turned around, smiling. "We watched—"

"I know exactly what movie you watched and it's time the male Dorothy gets out of that outfit."

Blake harrumphed an unintelligible reply and clomped clumsily to the bedroom, slamming the door loudly. Then from behind the door, he said, "And to think, I shaved my legs for this."

Chapter 18

Alex sat on the loveseat in the study, her long legs tucked under her, voraciously drinking in every word of JJ's first novel, while JJ wrote.

"How romantic," Alex said aloud, as she sighed. JJ looked up momentarily and smiled. If there were any doubts left about the identity of these characters, they were fading, even though she still found the situation unbelievable.

She then glanced at Blake. With his one knee crossed over another, he had buried himself in a tome on the Civil War. True to her description of him, he appeared to be constantly in search of knowledge.

The jangle of the landline on the desk interrupted her thoughts and startled Alex, causing her to spring out of her seat like a jack in the box.

"I'll get it." Alex quickly took the few steps to grab the receiver.

"Oh, no, you don't. I'm still recovering from the last time you answered my phone," she said, as she reached for it. Alex sighed again and returned to the loveseat.

"Deb, what a surprise." They chatted briefly before Deb said Dr. Chare wanted to speak with her. "Really? Sure, I'll wait." She wondered why he was calling.

"Why, Dr. Chare, what a pleasure to hear your voice again. My favorite history department chairman. What a surprise." Her days at the department rippled through her memory.

While she talked, Alex sat on the edge of her seat.

"Teach? You'd like me to teach this term." Her mind quickly shot to Kennedy King Cooper.

"No, no, I couldn't possibly do that." She paused. *And be anywhere near that snob.*

"No, really, Thom. If there were some way I could, I certainly would." *How about your kicking that Cooper jerk out? Then we could talk.*

"I have a deadline coming up." Again, a pause.

"You did? I didn't have you pegged for the romantic type. Oh, you did it mostly because I wrote it? How sweet. Well, I'm glad you enjoyed it."

Another pause.

"I realize Dr. Kalinger's illness straps you and you're short on teaching staff. But I'm sure there is some young, eager new graduate out there waiting for the position, just dying to get the experience."

Yet another pause. With every pause, Alex leaned forward a fraction of inch more. If she leaned farther, she would fall of the couch.

"No, I really can't. You see, I've also got—" *now, how did Blake describe them* "—my cousin and her fiancé from…"

"Kansas." Blake filled in the dead air, only momentarily taking his attention off the book.

"Uh, Kansas," she repeated the prompting into the phone.

She chatted with the chair a few more minutes. "Yes, I promise. If I change my mind, I'll call you. But don't hold your breath."

She replaced the receiver on its cradle and said, "Good God, that was close. For a while I didn't think he was going to take no for an answer."

Alex gave her a quizzical look. "Did you just turn down an offer to teach in the same department that Professor Cooper teaches," she asked, shaking her head.

"Yeah, I did. He asked me to fill in for a professor who was going to be out the entire term because of an illness."

"Why didn't you say yes?" Alex asked.

"Precisely because of Cooper. The last thing I need is to come face to face with him on a daily basis."

Alex shot off the couch. "Let me get this straight. You had a chance to fulfill your destiny and you purposely threw it away?" She went pale, waving her hands frantically. "Don't you know love never knocks twice?"

She shook her head, laughing.

"What? What's so funny?"

"You. Where did you get that corny phrase 'love never knocks twice'? It sounds like the title of a romance novel."

Alex stopped dead in her tracks, her entire countenance changed.

"That's because it is. I read it last night. It was on the nightstand in our bedroom. And just for your information, it was a grand love story."

"Love isn't knocking at all." JJ shook her head.

Blake peered out from behind his book.

"Technically this would have been the third encounter for the pair. The more appropriate response would have been third time's the charm."

"Blake." The women said together.

"Well, it is." He quickly returned to reading.

"You mean Cooper's the only reason you turned

down that offer?"

"Of course. Otherwise, I would have been more than willing to help Chare out. He's been so very kind to me. He defended my book to the academic community—risking his own reputation, I might add—when he didn't have to. This is actually a small favor he's asking in return. Except for the presence of Cooper." She glanced at the time on the computer.

"Shoot, I'm supposed to meet Nan at the Physics Café for coffee. I'm running late." She powered down her computer and shot up out of her chair. As she rushed to get her keys from the holder by the back door, she called, "Try to behave today, please."

****

Alex waited to hear the back door shut.

"Come on. Now's our chance."

"Our chance to do what?" He looked up from the book.

"To go to the university and get this Chare guy to ask JJ to teach again."

Blake put down the book. "Weren't you listening? He's already asked her to teach again. The lady said no."

She nodded, pulling him off the couch. "I believe it was one of your distinguished bards who wrote 'The lady doth protest too much.' "

As he got dragged to his feet, he said, "It's interesting that you should use that particular phrase, because most people quote that wrong. That comes from Hamlet, by the way, and Queen…"

"Blake."

"What?"

"I don't care about the history of the quote right now. We need to get JJ teaching at the university so we

75

can get her and Cooper together long enough to know they were made for each other."

"Are you not listening to me? She's already—"

"A mere technicality, I assure you."

"And we're going to the university and do what?"

She stared him directly in the eyes, as if the answer were right in front of him. "What are we going to do? Well, I haven't figured that part out yet. But guaranteed we'll do something."

As she dragged him through the kitchen, he asked another question.

"I hate to mention this, but we have no vehicle. How are we going to get to the university?"

"But we do have a car. It's sitting out in the garage. And I'm betting the keys"—she paused, searching the hook where all of JJ's keys hung in the kitchen—"are right here."

Triumphantly, she picked out a set of keys.

"How do you know there's another car in the garage?"

She chuckled.

"What's so humorous about that question?"

"Nothing but the answer, sweetheart. I saw the car the day you threw me over the deck railing to save me from the fire. The car, I'm betting, is her late husband's. I don't suppose he'll mind much if we use it."

Chapter 19

Though Blake was thoroughly convinced the trip to the university was nothing but wasted effort, he felt a wave of excitement well up in him at the prospect of leaving the house.

"Road trip," he shouted, shaking his head from side to side, his hair tousling about in response. He snatched the keys from Alex and ran for the door to the garage. "I'm driving."

He opened it and stood momentarily paralyzed, his mouth hanging open in amazement.

"You've got to be kidding me. This isn't a car; this is a wind-up toy." The compact car was the smallest he'd seen in his life.

"Baby, we don't have a choice. If we expect to get our mission accomplished in this world, then we need to use whatever means it takes."

"Even if it means I have to fold my legs eleven times in order to fit in that thing?"

"Exactly. I'm glad to see you're getting into the spirit of helping JJ."

He shook his head as he opened the car door. He scrutinized the space—or lack of it—as he tried to size up how he would squeeze his tall frame into the vehicle. He finally climbed in, carefully dragging and arranging his legs in what little space there was.

"Ow. Who was this thing made for? Munchkins?"

"What did you say? I can't understand you." Then she giggled. "I think it has something to do with your knees knocking on your chin when you speak."

"I find no humor in the situation."

He took a good look around him to familiarize himself with all the knobs and controls of the car. Puzzled, he quickly turned to Alex who had climbed into the other side.

She smiled. Her right hand extended outward palm out. "Keys, please." She gave a happy little shrug.

"You're not in London anymore. You're sitting on the passenger side. And I know you don't want to go through that whole process of getting out and then getting back in on this side. It's just easier if you give me the keys."

Deflated and defeated, he handed over the keys. "But I get to drive home."

"Of course, sweetheart. Sure." She inserted the key into the ignition, put the car in reverse and backed out of the garage. His spirits buoyed.

She suddenly stopped. "There's only one slight flaw in my plan. I'm not exactly sure where I'm going." She placed her head on the steering wheel. "Okay, I don't have a clue about where I'm headed."

"Don't worry about that. I'm already taking care of it. Geeps knows how to get us there."

"Geeps?"

"Yeah, look right here." He pointed to a small digital screen in the middle of the dashboard. "I just programmed in the University of Northern Ohio as our destination."

The voice spoke. Turn left onto North Pine Boulevard.

"Ooohhh, a GPS system."

"Yeah, that's what I said, 'Geeps.' Let's get going. If I stay in this car too long, I'll never be able to unfold my legs again."

Once they got on North Pine Boulevard, Geeps took them four blocks. They made another left on Empire Road and then after several miles a right onto Albert Street.

The pair found themselves in the middle of the old industrial center of Bell Wyck. Alex looked bewildered at first. She stared at the aging, rusting empty buildings on one side of the road and the boarded up storefronts on the other. Her eyes got red. Tears ran down her cheeks.

"What's wrong, love?"

"Look at it. Just look at it. It looks more like a war zone than a city. How could anyone live around here? It's depressing."

She waved a hand at the scenery. "It's really the first time I've ever seen anything like this. JJ didn't write depressing scenes like this in our world. Everything where we come from is beautiful."

He had to agree. Even he was taken aback by the stark reality of a rusting, deserted Midwest factory town. He had no words to describe it himself.

"It is disturbing," he finally managed to say.

Quickly, Geeps guided them off that road. Immediately, Alex's mood seemed to brighten.

"I didn't realize how lucky we are to have JJ shielding us from that. It only makes me more determined to help her find the happiness she deserves."

They finally arrived at the college and found the history department. After a few inquiries, they located the office.

"Excuse me." Alex twirled a strand of her hair as she measured her next words. "But I was wondering…" She flashed her eyes at Blake.

"You're the one who said we were going to tell the truth."

Alex winced at the reminder.

The receptionist looked up from her computer. "May I help you?"

Alex hesitated so Blake jumped right in—ready to tell The Truth. Their perspective of it, at least.

"Why, yes you can." Then he looked around. "But is there somewhere a little more private we can speak? Where random people would be less likely to walk in on us?"

At that moment, a balding, older man emerged from a nearby office and approached with a stack of folders. He acknowledged their presence.

"Excuse me. I just want to steal Deb for one minute. Here are potential candidates to fill in for Dr. Kalinger this term. He won't be able to return. Please call these to see how many are available and schedule them for an interview with me as soon as possible."

As the man turned to go, the receptionist replied, "Wouldn't JJ be the logical choice?"

She quirked an eyebrow. He laughed.

"Don't even play that game with me, Deb. I know darn well you listened in on my conversation with JJ earlier this morning. And you know she said no."

He turned to them and thanked them for their patience. Once again, he turned to go, but stopped and gave them another look.

"Either of you have college teaching experience? I'm looking for a good prof for this term. The best just turned me down."

"Sir," Alex spoke up. The man turned his attention toward her. "You must be Dr. Chare."

He nodded. "Actually, that's why we're here—about JJ."

"Oh?"

"This is a little difficult to explain. And she would kill us if she knew we were here. But we really think she should be teaching this term. We think that it would, uh—"

Blake jumped in. "We think it would not only refresh her skills at teaching, but the change would enhance her creativity as well."

Chare smiled. He looked to Deb who simply shrugged.

"Okay, let's take this into my office. Deb, I have a feeling you should come in, too. This sounds like some type of conspiracy that's going to need your devious mind. And, of course, I mean that as a compliment."

The four of them entered his office and he closed the door. He beckoned them to sit as he sat behind his large mahogany desk.

"I'm not buying the enhancing of creativity. So just tell me straight. First, who are and what are you up to?"

Alex stammered, so Blake jumped in, even though he had little faith in the idea. He laid all the cards, well, almost all of them—on the table.

He introduced them as JJ's cousin and fiancé from Kansas. Then set the scene for Chare and Debbie. "So, you see, JJ needs to take this position in order to force her to interact with Professor Cooper. I realize, sir, that matchmaking isn't normally part of your job description, but you've also already admitted she's the best candidate for the job."

Alex finally spoke. "You'd be accomplishing two very worthwhile goals. You'd have the best person working in the position. And, as an added bonus, you'd have the satisfaction of helping a loving relationship blossom."

At that Deb broke into laughter. "It's anything but loving yet, from the way Professor Cooper acts."

"Yeah, JJ hasn't realized yet that he really is the man of her dreams. It may take a little more interaction with him on a regular basis. You do know that's the premise of all the great love stories," she said as she sighed.

Dr. Chare leaned back in his large leather desk chair, carefully stroking his head with his hand.

"This is real life, young lady, not some fictional love story you're dealing with."

"Yes, sir. I'm keenly aware of the difference between the events of a romance novel and real life."

"Wasn't it Oscar Wilde," Blake asked, "who said life imitates art far more than art imitates life?"

The small group fell silent. Chare scratched his head.

"Dr. Chare," Alex said, "I believe there is chemistry between JJ and Professor Cooper. It's just going to take time."

"This is not within the realm of a department chair. My job is not to worry about romances between professors. Let alone be complicit in fostering them."

Alex slumped in her chair. Blake reached for her hand. He was ready to offer words of consolation, when Chare spoke.

"Debbie, get JJ back on the phone. Tell her every other candidate has already been grabbed up by another school or is unavailable to teach. Heck, you're the creative liar of the group. Tell her anything, but make sure she's here in time next week to teach the nine a.m. Historical Conspiracy class that is team taught. Just try to avoid the words 'team taught' and above all don't mention that Kenn Cooper will be her partner." He sounded like a general gathering and commanding his troops for combat.

He raised an eyebrow as he turned his attention toward Alex and Blake. "How does that work for you?"

Alex rose to leave. "Thank you so much."

Blake jumped up, took Chare's hand, and pumped it vigorously.

"Thank you, sir. Thank you very much." He paused.

"Is there something else, young man?"

"Why, yes, if it wouldn't be too much trouble?" And then he posed his question, causing the chair to chortle.

"Yes, if JJ agrees to this, I certainly can arrange for that. It would be the least that I could do."

****

The chair stood as the three of them left the room. Once alone, he slumped into his seat, wondering what he had just done.

"Well, at least it's for a good cause. Young love."

Then he pulled out his copy of JJ's second book, *Love's Revenge,* opened it to where his bookmark lay, and continued to read.

Chapter 20

Kenn panicked when he heard his mother was on line one. And when he heard the click of Deb's receiver leaving him hanging, he felt as if he were going to have a panic attack.

It's not that he didn't love his mother. He did. But he knew what awaited him on the other side of that telephone. He didn't have the emotional energy to deal with it. He was still recovering from the surprise dinner party. But the line wouldn't stop blinking at him.

Suck it up. He raised the receiver to his ear and pushed line one. "Hi, Mom."

"Son, so good to hear from you. Remember Sofie Addelmyer?" His mom wasted no words on small talk.

"No, Mom, and hello to you, too."

"Sofie and you sat next to each other in the first grade, in Mrs. Brown's class."

"Are you talking about the mean girl with the frizzy blonde hair who always kicked me when we went out to recess? That Sofie Addelmyer? The one who wore those horrible-looking pink glasses with glitter?" *Could there possibly be two Sofie Addelmyers in this world?*

"Yes, hon, she's the one," Mrs. Cooper said without skipping a beat. "Well, I saw her mother at Zingo's supermarket the other day. And she's a reference librarian in Wilmington, Delaware.

"Well, her mom and I thought we'd get you two kids

together. It seems like the perfect match, the reference librarian and the historian."

"Why? So she can kick me when I ask for a historic document she thought I shouldn't see?"

"Oh, honey, she's an adult now, she wouldn't kick you. Get over it."

"I'll pass on Sofie."

Mrs. Cooper continued to protest. Kenn, though, was in no mood to humor his mother's misplaced zeal.

"Mom, why do you continue to do this to me?" he asked, exasperated with his mother's continuous attempts at finding him the right woman.

"Do what?"

"You know what. This." He waved his hand, even though he knew his mother couldn't see the motion.

"If you really want to know, I'll tell you," she said, "but you won't like the answer."

"Tell me, anyway," he sighed.

"Honey, the last couple of women you chose really weren't suited for you. Yes, they were beautiful, but they weren't women you could make a lasting relationship with." She paused, but for only a split second.

"Take that last one, for instance. What was her name, Shower, Breeze—"

"Rain. Her name was Rain." He felt his muscles tighten.

"Now, really, what kind of name is that?"

"Mom, stop. I get the idea. I haven't made good choices. But it's my life and my mistakes." He could tell by the silence at the other end that he had wounded his mother.

"Mom, I really didn't have a good weekend. And I'm running late to class." *Okay, so that last part was a lie—she was in Boston, she didn't know the term hadn't started yet.*

"You know I love you, Mom. I'll try to make it home for at least a weekend soon. Bye." He clicked down the receiver as quickly as he could.

Damn. She's irritating as all hell. But the woman is right. My choices in women have been disastrous. And Rain. She left me for some old fogey on a motorcycle on the pretense of doing research for her sociological doctorate. Yeah, right.

So, what's wrong with me, he thought. *I finally find someone who I have something in common with and I push her away because of a difference of opinion on her taste in literature. Why would I do that? What kind of self-sabotaging jerk am I?*

****

"But Deb, I've already said no. There's no possible way I can teach right now." JJ was in her home office struggling with a paragraph. Ever since the arrival of her characters, she found it difficult to work on their book. Especially when they would sit on the loveseat across from her, like they were at the moment.

"I'm working on this novel and it's just not moving forward as quickly as I had planned." *And then there's the issue of that idiot of a professor you have in the department. And I have two unexpected characters staying with me. But let's not go there.*

"You cannot tell me that there is no other person who can teach this term." She rubbed the back of her neck.

"Two classes. That's all you have to teach. A few hours out of a day. The rest of the day is yours. The chair's desperate. He's depending on you to say yes."

Deb paused. "And you know, he was there for you when you needed an ally in the department."

"Dammit, don't remind me. That's just not fair of you to bring that up." Deb didn't reply. The silence hung in the air.

Inhaling deeply and audibly exhaling, she recognized when she was beaten. "All right. What times are the classes?"

She shook her head in disbelief as she wrote the class times down. Hanging up the phone, she worried what she had gotten herself into. "Dammit."

What Deb said was true. She knew she owed Dr. Chare. He was one of the few in the department who believed she could research and write to academic standards on conspiracy theories. He had given her every advantage possible. But more than that he had fought hard and persuaded the others on her panel to accept the final dissertation. It was because of him she had her doctorate.

He had been a second father to her through that entire process. Not only was he a staunch defender of her abilities, he also displayed a sincere interest in her as a person. How many times did they talk when she thought the pressures were trapping her in an emotional cage? He knew how to put the situation, whatever it was, in perspective. That encouragement allowed her to refocus her efforts on the important work of research and writing.

If it weren't for the chair, she knew that she would not be where she was today. Yeah, she decided that facing the possibility of running into Cooper was worth the price of helping him. It was the least she could do.

Who was she fooling? It wasn't just a *possibility* that she would run into Cooper. *It was a certainty.* She just had to be mature about the matter and deal with it.

Alex calmly looked up from the magazine she was reading. "Something wrong?"

"I have just been guilted into teaching this term. Not fair. Not fair at all."

She stood up, and, using what little room she had in her office, paced.

"Okay, it's not going to be as bad as I think it will be," she said, talking more to herself than her houseguests. She chewed on her lower lip, as she furrowed her eyebrows. *Oh, God, it couldn't be.*

"I just have to go on campus, teach, hold short"— the writer stopped in mid-stride, whirled around at what seemed like lightning speed, and looked Alex in the face, shaking both index fingers at her, emphasized—"and I mean short office hours. Then I'm home."

She continued to pace. "And all the while pray that I don't run into or even get a glimpse of that Kennedy Cooper."

Just the thought of seeing him again resurrected the sexual feelings she had when she sat way too close to him at Nan's.

The feelings—no, admitting to the feelings— frightened her. If she were honest, she'd confess she took notice of him long before she bumped into him. *Okay, I saw him walk in and thought…*JJ stopped there.

She stopped pacing. "Aghh!"

Blake and Alex looked up at her and then at each other, exchanging smiles. Alex deliberately set the magazine aside and asked, "What's wrong?"

"Nothing. Nothing at all. I'm going to take a cold shower. I'll be back."

Chapter 21

Memories flooded JJ as she wended her way across the quad of University of Northern Ohio toward Mundain Hall, the home of the history department. The tree-lined quad, the old stately buildings, imposingly sprinkled around the green expanse, the traffic of students swiftly changing classes, lugging the ubiquitous backpacks created a flashback to her graduate days. And then there were the squirrels—both brown and black— that dotted and dodged the quad, resembling windup toys sprung too tightly. They reminded her of the many times she had shared her outdoor lunch with them.

She not only earned her doctorate at this university, but she also had taught here for several years. In so many ways it had been home—and probably always would be in her heart.

That was due mostly because of the chair. And that, she told herself, was the only reason she was back. *The only reason I'm risking another chance encounter with that impossible man. I'm only doing it for Dr. Chare.*

Keep telling yourself that, kiddo. You're not doing it because you're the least bit curious about the extent of the chemistry you think Kenn Cooper and you may have. No, not at all. Don't acknowledge your femininity, your sexual needs, and your ultimate need to be loved for who you are. Nope. None of that played a role in the decision. Sure, keep telling yourself that.

She was so lost in her thoughts, she didn't see the couple crossing the quad in the opposite direction and bumped into them.

"I'm so sorry," JJ said. "Are you okay?"

"We're fine," the woman said. "It was our fault. We're trying to get to the psychology department. Could you point us in the right direction?"

JJ took a double take at the couple. They looked like they had time traveled from the 1960s. The woman wore a peasant blouse and a long paisley-printed skirt. A peace-sign dangled around her neck. The man looked even more out of place, with hair tightly curled and a tie-dyed shirt as was the fashion a half century ago. Both wore reflective aviator sunglasses.

Then the two hippie-clad characters suddenly looked horrified and peered over their shades at the same time. They looked at each other and sprinted away.

"Such odd behavior," she said out loud. You don't see students dressed like that every day, she thought, thinking about the hippie vibe. She turned around to give them one last look. At the same moment they turned to catch one last glimpse of her.

"They look strangely familiar," she said. "But I just can't put my finger on it. I wonder if I know them from somewhere. They remind me of…"

It was now her turn to look shocked and horrified. "No, it couldn't be," she assured herself, "it just couldn't be them."

Once across the quad, she tried to clear her mind. She put aside the past and pushed the dread she felt about the possibility of running into Cooper aside and concentrated only on the present.

She found the department's office to be much like

she remembered. Deb sat at her desk, working at the computer and no doubt screening the chair's calls as well as his visitors. The bank of faculty mailboxes was on the far wall, along with several copies of the school newspaper, *The Daily Digit,* on a table.

After making small talk with Deb and greeting Dr. Chare like a long-lost parent, she got her room assignments.

"The first class," Deb explained, "is in Room 134, right down the hall here, but you know where that is. And I've put the syllabus in there already. You should feel right at home. One of the texts for the course is your book." Deb paused. "When you're done with classes, I'll show you to your office. I think you'll like it."

She thanked Deb and headed for her first class, chuckling. This would be different. She had never used her own book as an assigned reading before.

She walked into the classroom and saw him, Kennedy King Cooper.

"What are you doing here? This is my class."

"No, this is a team-taught course." He paused and ran a hand through his hair. "And you cannot possibly be my partner. Because my partner is the author of this text." He pointed to the book on the desk. "J. Jordan St. Clair."

She purposely chose to ignore that comment. "Deb just now assigned me to this room. She said nothing about it being a team teaching this course. Whose harebrained scheme was this?"

"It was my harebrained scheme, professors." Thom Chare stood in the doorway. She and Kenn pivoted. "And I do believe it's a brilliant harebrained scheme," he added.

The chair apparently enjoyed the silence that followed.

"Kenn, I see you've met Dr. St. Clair. I'm confident you two are destined to make an incredibly powerful impact on the young minds in this room." His voice was calm and clear. Again, he paused.

"Now, suck it up and get on with the teaching." And with that he disappeared.

She and Kenn exchanged looks. He was the first to speak.

"You're J. Jordan St. Clair? But how can that be? I always thought he was a…"

"Male, right?"

"Well, yeah."

She knew she should be furious. And maybe later she would be. But somehow that seemed unimportant right now. Sure, the astonished look on his face gave her a smug satisfaction, but she suddenly felt sorry for the man.

"Hey," she nudged him. *Damn. Mistake to touch him. Make mental note to keep a distance.*

"Look, we've got an audience," she said loudly. The class laughed. "They're expecting a show. One that centers around history. Controversial and conspiratorial history."

Then she addressed the class. "I'm Professor St. Clair, but you've probably already figured that one out. This is Professor Kennedy King Cooper. We're you're historical guides for this course."

"You're not Dr. St. Clair," one student called out. "You're JJ Spritely, the romance author. I've read all your books." Several other students loudly agreed. Her presence caused a stir of excitement among many of the female students.

She felt her cheeks grow hot. The last time she taught, she didn't have to deal with this. She hadn't been a published novelist yet.

Kenn deftly jumped in. "True enough, she is. But prior to that, she established herself as a reputable, accomplished historian. So, when you go to open your text for this class later on tonight, you know it won't be boring. But I'll give you one hint. When it comes to the Marilyn Monroe-JFK conspiracy theory, don't expect a happily-ever-after ending."

The class laughed. He had said the perfect words to put everyone, especially herself, at ease. And she was grateful.

"Now, let's get down to business, shall we? We've got a lot of ground to cover. Because some people"—he took a step away from her and with a flourish pointed to her—"see conspiracies lurking behind every event."

She curtsied flamboyantly. "It's true," she said, then flashed Kenn a smile. "I may not agree with some of them one-hundred percent—"

"Excuse me, professors." They pivoted at the exact same moment. It was the chair again.

"I have two more late registering additions to your class." Behind him stood two figures who looked as if they just emerged from a recently unearthed time capsule from the 1960s. The couple she had bumped into on the quad.

"Peace, man," he said as he flashed two fingers in the "V" formation. "Right on!" He raised a clenched fist.

"Gone with the wind," said the woman standing next to him. Her partner nudged her. "That's go with the flow," he coached.

"Yeah, go with the flow. Tune in, turn out—and jump in."

Chare hurriedly made the introductions through his chuckling. "Here are your two new students. A little late, but better late than never. Here are the proper registration forms."

Her jaw dropped and her eyes widened. Now that she got a closer look at them, she realized her first impulse of who they were was right.

It was all she could do to not explode. She caught Blake by the arm as the character hurriedly tried to get past her. "What are you two doing here?" she whispered through clenched teeth.

"Dr. Chare is most certainly a man of his word. He's paying our tuition this term as a thank you for our part in getting you to teach."

"Blake!"

Alex hit him from behind with a three-ring notebook. Blake stumbled forward several paces. As furious as she was at the two, she couldn't help but notice the sticker on the binder proclaimed, "Make love, not war."

"Oops." Blake evidently realized his enormous gaffe. The young Brit ran to take a seat in the auditorium-style classroom. Alex hurriedly followed.

"You two are in big trouble," JJ said as they tried to hide in their seats. She sounded more like a mom than she had intended. "And take that ridiculous wig off."

"I can't, Dr. JJ," Blake said, "This ridiculous wig is my own hair."

"I gave him a home permanent late last night to celebrate our first day of school," Alex said as she gazed at him.

94

"Oh, my Lord."

The rest of the class, which had been mesmerized watching this unorthodox scene, immediately burst into laughter. Even Kenn, who had remained in the shadows throughout all of this, roared. It took him a few moments to catch his breath.

She didn't have time to deal with them at the moment. Kenn, who finally composed himself, was already attempting to steer the class back into the course, thank God. She needed to keep up with him.

The two presented the syllabus, then immediately dug into the material. They discovered a natural cadence in their teaching styles, using humor to highlight fundamental differences in their individual interpretations. She, naturally purposely led the class toward a conspiratorial view, while Kenn interjected his objection, along with sound historical evidence, with impeccable timing. The result was an entertaining and educational glimpse into a seldom-studied segment of history.

Then with perfect timing, the pair wrapped up the session and reviewed the reading assignment for the next session. Just as they finished, the bell rang. The class broke out in applause. Both professors looked astonished.

"Bravo. Bravo," came a voice from the door. It was the chair.

Chapter 22

"Oh, my goodness." JJ walked into her newly assigned office and stopped in the middle of the room. She whirled around in a full circle, like a little girl showing off a new skirt.

"It's the same office. The same office I had when I taught here before. How did the chair arrange that?"

She tossed her briefcase on one of the two receiving chairs in front of her large oak desk and scanned the room.

Nothing had changed. Of course, what did she really expect to be different? The large old bookcase still stood across from the desk—now her desk, at least temporarily. It held no books at the moment. She vowed to change that soon. She looked out the large windows to her right, pleased with the view of the majestic old maple tree spreading its branches. Yes, the chair had taken good care of her. He, indeed, was grateful for her teaching this term.

She walked behind the desk and sat down. "Wow, even the same chair. I loved this chair." It was one of those great chairs that had arms and it swiveled. She sat down. She forgot about her now-living characters, and she forgot about Kenn. She twirled in her chair. Again and again. Just like a child. And for the moment, she really did feel childlike. And she liked it. A lot.

"Knock, knock."

It took a second for the voice to register with her, and by the time it did, it was too late. She stopped abruptly. There stood Kenn, with a faint smile that gradually changed into a wide boyish grin.

"I see you enjoy a good chair." His deep brown eyes twinkled. "May I come in for a moment?"

"You caught me." Instead of being irritated at his apparent amusement, she grinned back. "Some kids never grow up," she confessed.

"Sit down, please." Did she just invite him to sit and make himself comfortable? The man she vowed she would have no contact with while she taught?

Her teaching partner readily accepted her offer, sat down in the remaining available seat across from her desk, crossed his legs at the knees, and appeared to make himself quite comfortable, as if they had been lifelong friends. She was amused at how quickly he settled in.

"You seemed to recognize those last two students Dr. Chare brought in. The two time travelers? They certainly are a colorful pair."

"Yes, they are. If you only knew how colorful they really can be."

"I could imagine."

"Oh, no you can't. I assure you."

"Just out of idle curiosity, how do you know them?"

She wondered if she was going to be judged guilty through association, even though the question sounded innocent enough.

"They're two characters…" She stopped. She was about to say in her novel, but thankfully realized how insane that would sound.

"Yes, they certainly are a couple of characters, I agree. I think Blake—is that his name?" She nodded. "I

97

believe he will be a very active and vocal student."

"That wouldn't surprise me in the least," she said softly. Even though she wanted to avoid the question, she knew she had to explain the relationship somehow. So, she resorted to the cousins-from-Kansas cover.

"That's not the real reason I stopped by, though. I'd like to, uhm, well…" Kenn uncrossed his legs and put his elbows on his knees.

She was surprised at his apparent loss for words. In her few encounters with him he always seemed to be at ease making conversation, and certainly not shy about speaking his mind. He squirmed in the chair like a schoolboy waiting to see the principal.

"Oh, darn it. There's no other way to say it." He looked her in the eyes. "I'm sorry."

He paused, leaving her to wonder momentarily what he was sorry for.

"When I first met you, I really did judge you by your appearance and your profession. I didn't think a woman as good looking as you who wrote romance novels would be interested in history, let alone be a professor."

She felt her cheeks grow hot with embarrassment. She wasn't sure how to answer him. She just heard him say she was good looking. Imagine that. And he admitted she was bright.

It had been a long time since any man had given her a compliment, especially someone as engaging as he. Did she just call him engaging? She gave herself a mental slap. *No, I can't think of him like that.*

He leaned back in his chair as if he were relieved he had actually said what was on his mind. Without waiting for her to accept the apology, he changed the subject.

"I'm looking forward to seeing what the next

session brings to our class," he said. She got the feeling he was stalling, that he had something else on his mind other than the class. She could tell by the way he continued to look into her eyes. No one had looked at her like that since her husband died. There was a lot for her to handle in this seemingly unassuming meeting. While she realized she couldn't compare Kenn to Geoff, this man had a boyish charisma all his own she had to work hard to ignore.

"I was wondering if—" he continued.

Just then, his cell phone rang. He quickly looked at it and groaned.

"Obviously someone you'd prefer not to talk to."

"My mother," he said, wincing.

"You know you can't ignore Mom."

He sighed deeply and answered the call. She noticed he quickly sat up straighter in his chair, using perfect posture when talking with his mother.

"Hi, Mom."

"Kenn, I have bad news. Sofie Addelmyer just got engaged."

The volume on his phone was loud enough JJ could hear what his mother said.

"To some accountant from Wilmington, Delaware. I know you're heartbroken dear, but—"

"Mom, I'm kind of busy here."

"—but there's hope, sweetheart. I just ran into little Mary Margaret O'Mally's mom at a fund raiser. And she isn't dating."

"Mom. No. Please. I can't talk right now. I'm having a conversation with my new teaching partner. Her name is JJ Spritely."

Mrs. Cooper fell silent. "Mom, are you there?"

"She's never speechless," he whispered to JJ.

"I heard that."

"I thought you left me."

"You couldn't be so lucky. But for a moment I thought you said you were with JJ Spritely."

"I did."

"Not the JJ Spritely." JJ could her his mom's comment, and she felt her cheeks get hot.

"I don't know. How do you know JJ Spritely?"

"Well, personally, I don't. But my book club has just finished her latest work, *Love's Revenge*." She paused, then gave a disappointed sigh and said, "No, it couldn't be *that* JJ Spritely."

She enjoyed Kenn's bewilderment. "Uhm, I don't know. Let me ask her." He moved forward so he was sitting on the edge of the chair. Moving the cell phone from his ear, he held it out so his mom could hear and asked, "Is *Love's Revenge* your latest book?"

He motioned to her to talk loud enough so his mom could listen in. "Yes, Mrs. Cooper, that is my latest book."

"Kenn, let me talk to her right now, and don't you dare tell your mother no."

He rolled his eyes and panic flooded his face. JJ, however, remained calm and motioned for him to give her the phone. She enjoyed the moment tremendously.

"Oh, really? Well, thank you. Oh, you are? Well, I'm not sure. Oh, I see."

She gave her teaching partner an amused look and shrugged her shoulders as she continued to listen.

"Why, of course, I'd be delighted to do that. Sure, I'll get that from Kenn." She ended the call and handed the phone back to him.

"What was that all about?"

"Two things: Your lack of a love life and an autographed copy of my book."

Hearing the words love life he shrank as deeply into the chair as he could. It wasn't difficult to sense his embarrassment, so laughingly, she said, "You'll have to give me her address. She's a fan."

He straightened up a little with that comment. "Is everyone a fan?"

"According to my royalty checks and several reviews I've read, no, if that comforts you at all."

"I did come in for one other reason," Kenn continued, apparently determined to remain on track. "I was hoping—"

Chapter 23

"Uno, uno, uno! We're number one!" Enthusiastic voices echoed throughout the hallway.

Kenn looked toward the door. A group of young men, one of whom was dressed as the football team's mascot, trooped around like soldiers on a five-mile hike. Following close behind were the men's backup singers—a group of lightly clad cheerleaders. All were festooned in the school colors of purple and lime green. And Alex was among them.

When the group arrived at JJ's door, the mascot stopped. Not expecting the sudden end of the march, the rest of the pep squad bumped into one another, causing a domino effect. The cheerleaders then crashed into them.

The mascot, a six-foot tall hand with the index finger pointed upward, indicating the Number One, casually said, "Hi, JJ."

The costume muffled the voice, but there was no mistaking that English accent. Blake.

"See, I told you I knew JJ Spritely, the romance author," Alex said. "She's my cousin."

The mascot took the top knuckle off the extended index finger revealing his head. The static electricity created by the headpiece made his hair a worse mop of a tangled mess than it usually was. Einstein's frightened hair looked manageable by comparison.

Seeing who was in the costume, Kenn bubbled up

with laughter. JJ gave him what she hoped he understood to be a don't-encourage-him look. But, evidently, seeing her open annoyance only made the situation that much more outlandish. His natural reaction to the comical situation started her laughing as well. Blake feigned indignation.

"I've got to go," Kenn said, barely able to speak he was laughing so hard. He made his way through the group of approximately a dozen young men like Moses parting the Red Sea and walked away. Part of her mourned his departure. They were actually talking civilly to each other, and she liked it.

Blake's new friends, all members of the university's men's pep squad, also dispersed quickly. So did Alex's fellow cheerleaders.

"See you at practice," Alex told one, as they exchanged hugs. She walked into the office and Blake followed her. But his attention was on his love and not where he was going.

Bam. The three folded fingers on the side of the costume hit the doorway and buffeted him to the other side, where the thumb portion of the outfit promptly scraped it.

"Not to worry," he said. "Not. To. Worry." He sidled unsteadily sideways into the office, thumb first.

He bent to sit in the chair. He couldn't. Part of his outfit might have fit, but the rest of it, the actual palm of the hand and those darned curled fingers, extended beyond the arm of the chair. He struggled and finally placed his headpiece on the desk so he could maneuver a little easier. JJ stared at this head-sized fingernail realizing how disturbingly lifelike it was.

Meanwhile, Blake continued to try to wiggle the

palm and other fingers in under the arm of the chair. That didn't work. He got up, turned around, and stared at the chair, looking as if he were pleading for some help from it.

Both she and Alex found his stance ridiculous and laughed.

"No one informed me of the hazards of the job before I signed on to be Ulysses Uno."

"Ulysses?" She couldn't help but laugh even more. "You mean this finger actually has a name? In all my years here, I never realized he had a name."

"I was told the student body just recently voted on it," Blake said flatly. "It beat out Uriah quite handily."

"I bet it did."

Alex, meanwhile, had settled in her chair, and crossed her legs, making her short outfit look even shorter and accenting her shapely limbs.

"Look, I'm finally a cheerleader. I don't think I was ever one before. Was I?" She looked at JJ for guidance on her personal history.

She shook her head. "No, you never were."

Alex sat up taller in her chair and straightened her shoulders. JJ couldn't help but noticed how proud she was. Perhaps she should have made her one.

"We debut in two weeks at the football game," Blake said proudly. He had finally given up trying to sit. "Are you going to the game?" he asked.

He took Ulysses' head from JJ's desk, held it to his side as if it were in a military helmet, fingernail facing JJ, and stood next to Alex. He glanced over at the love of his life, dressed in such a tantalizing costume. JJ read his face and had no question about what the pair would be doing when they when they arrived home.

Chapter 24

"Do you hear that?" Kenn asked as he and JJ walked down the hall toward their classroom for the second session.

She nodded. "Sounds like it's coming from our classroom. And it doesn't sound good."

The moment she walked into the doorway she discovered how not good it was. It was like a Grade C science fiction movie: *The Attack of the Fans*.

"JJ, sign my book!"

"Ms. Spritely, sign mine first. I need to get to class!"

She faced what seemed like two dozen coeds, each armed with one of her novels, waving pens in the air pleading for an autograph. And they all swarmed around her like bees around a hive.

The group was so assertive and so determined they pushed Kenn aside to get as close to her as possible. Three to four young women at a time stuck books and pens in her face. Even if she wanted to sign the books, she couldn't. The wall of girls kept pushing her back. Having never been involved in such a scene, she was at a loss of what to do. *What if they start tearing my clothes off? No, they wouldn't do that. Would they?* She had never seen a group so resolute to get autographs.

At first, Kenn only watched the unbelievable scenario play out. After a few moments, he stepped in to quell the riot. He was able to maneuver the eager coeds away from the door by squeezing himself between her and several of the students closest to her. This let her actually enter the room. Then he announced that she would be delighted to do a book signing at the Physics Café at three p.m.

"Ladies, as much as Dr. St. Clair would love to take time now, we do have a history course to teach."

She looked at him nodding her approval and mouthed, "Good work. Thank you."

He winked at her. She thought her heart would melt. Then she chastised herself for having that reaction. *He is not my knight in shining armor.* But she was, indeed, grateful to him.

The mob scene was slowly breaking up. Some young ladies weren't pleased with being put off, but Kenn assured them that they would get individual time with JJ at the signing. That seemed to appease them, and they finally left.

Curiously, most of the students who accosted her were not even taking her course. Those who were reluctantly took their seats.

"Thanks, that was quick thinking on your part," she told Kenn once the front of the room cleared. "Now, all I need is a partner to join me at three to keep the peace. You seem to be perfect for the job." She wasn't quite sure why she blurted out this invitation. Except that she had a lingering, if baffling, need for him to join her. But she knew his thoughts on romance novels and novelists very well. She was sure he wouldn't willingly be a part of such a frivolous undertaking.

"Sure," he answered immediately. *Did I just see a glimpse of delight in those eyes?*

"I'd love to. But only under one condition."

"Oh, and what's that?"

"I finally get to buy you that coffee I offered when I met you at that book signing."

That disastrous meeting had all but faded from her memory. Chuckling, she answered. "I guess it's only fair. I was pretty hard on you that day."

The building's bell sounded signaling the start of class.

****

JJ and Kenn headed for the Physics Café about two thirty. Alex and Blake followed on Kenn's invitation (like they weren't going to tag along anyway). When the foursome arrived, they were stunned. A line of young women and a few men spewed out the door. It looked as if the café were giving something away.

The moment the four of them stepped in, Alvin rushed up to them. He was visibly frazzled. "It's about time you got here." He talked to JJ. "All these students said you were holding a book signing here. When I told them I didn't know anything about it, they were livid. I nearly had a riot on my hands."

Astonished, she looked around. The full impact of the situation struck her. Every booth and table was filled with young ladies tightly holding books. Here and there, she saw a man among them. She assumed they were coerced into attending.

"I really shouldn't complain," Alvin added. "Look, they're all buying something. This is going to be the best day yet for the store. I just wish I would have known you had planned this."

She explained she hadn't. "There were less than thirty people in the classroom when I agreed to this. I don't know how all of this happened." She scanned the café to take another look at the crowd.

As she turned, she caught Alex hurriedly shoving her cell phone into her pocket. "Alex?" She turned on a heel and came face-to-face with her character.

"Well, I just texted the other cheerleaders. When I told them I knew you, they told me how much they loved your books—"

"It's not completely her fault," Blake said, quietly. "I texted the men's pep squad and they spread the news to their girlfriends."

"Well, good work, guys," Alvin said. "JJ, I've got you all set up here at this table. And I'll bring three more chairs for the rest of you. And, yeah, order anything you want, all four of you. It's my treat."

She looked at Kenn as they strode over the table. "Guess you don't have to treat this time. That means you still owe me a coffee. I'm going to make sure you pay up, professor." *Did those words just come out of my mouth?*

"I'd be honored to buy such a renaissance woman not only coffee but a quiet meal as well. And I emphasize quiet."

Chapter 25

Alex nudged Blake in the ribs. "Ouch, what was that for?"

Kenn looked at the two. JJ glared at them.

"They're getting closer to becoming a couple, did you hear that?" Alex whispered. "Hopefully, that means we're getting closer to going home."

"Not before our first game." Blake panicked. "We've got duties here. Friends here."

"What do you mean? Wouldn't it be wonderful if it happened before that?"

"Of course, it would," he stammered. "But one date—one hypothetical date—doesn't make a romance. We still have our work cut out for us."

"I suppose you're right." She folded her arms and slumped in the chair.

"And then that's assuming that's why we're still here. I haven't stopped thinking of methods to get us home."

"That's what worries me," Alex said softly.

Just then, Alvin approached the pair. "Excuse me, but could I speak to you for a moment?"

Blake quirked an eyebrow. "Us?"

"Yes, I'd like to talk to both you and Alex." Blake shrugged as he and Alex slowly rose from their seats.

"Do you think we're in trouble?" Alex whispered.

"I'm not sure, love. He doesn't seem upset, just

serious." The owner led them to the kitchen. While not extremely quiet, the location did afford them some privacy from the crowd.

"I understand you're JJ's cousins."

"I am," Alex said brightly. "And Blake is my fiancé." She sighed as she said the word.

"And we're from Kansas."

"And you're taking courses at UNO and plan to stay a while?" Blake wondered where this line of questioning was headed.

"Actually," Alex began.

"Yes, we are," Blake said, "we like it here." Blake heard Alex whimper.

"What you did here today with absolutely no preparation is remarkable."

Alex looked puzzled. "What did we do?"

"You filled my café with paying customers in a matter of hours."

"When you look at it that way, I guess we did," Alex said.

"I'm impressed, very impressed." He paused. "Do you think you can duplicate your text marketing technique?"

"Text marketing?" For a moment, Blake had no idea what Alvin was talking about. Then it hit him. "You mean texting a group of people to plan the creation of an apparently spontaneous event?"

"Exactly!" the café owner exclaimed. He waved his hands as he talked. "If you even think you can, I'd like to hire you both as the café's new text marketing team.

"My partners and I are too busy running the café to get heavily involved in the marketing. But if you could produce this type of result, even once a month or so, I'd see to it that it was worth your time and effort."

Blake and Alex stole excited glances, each nodding yes. "Of course, we'd be glad to do. There's really nothing to it," Blake said. He straightened his shoulders back and thrust his chest out slightly. "A piece of pie."

"That's cake, darling. A piece of cake."

"Great." Alvin turned on a heel.

"Ted, Simon? Got a minute?" He waved to the two men standing across from each other at the work station. One of them had just finished adding croutons to a salad. The other had put the final touches on a sandwich order, which Blake thought looked delicious.

They approached them, still holding the food they had prepared, as Alvin made the introductions.

"This is Simon Quigley and Ted Quinn, my partners.

"Meet Blake and Alex. They're the individuals responsible for our tremendous business today." He paused. "And they've agreed to do the text marketing we talked about."

"That's great. You guys have a real gift for it." Simon passed the salad off to a food runner waiting to deliver it. Then he examined the cheesesteak sandwich. "Laura," he said, "it's ready to be de-particlized."

Laura, slim, short with dark hair pulled back in a ponytail, took the sandwich from him, placed it on the small work area in front of her and picked up what appeared to be a large super soaker water gun.

"What's that?" Blake asked.

"That's our de-particlizer. We use it on every Philadelphia Experiment Cheesesteak. We named the sandwich after the movie. You know the one. How the government attempted to de-particlize an entire aircraft carrier in World War II. One minute the ship was there, the next moment it was gone.

"Ted created this gun in his junior year of college. It's obviously not strong enough to make an aircraft carrier disappear. But sometimes we get lucky. We turn it on the sandwich. It's supposed to de-particlize the onions. It just doesn't always work when we want it to. Sometimes there's a delayed effect. If you get a sandwich with onions and they disappear while you're eating it, you get a free cappuccino."

Alex appeared a bit wary of the contraption, but Blake walked right up to the employee using it to get a closer look. "Any chance of trying this baby out?"

"Sorry, no. You have to be trained to use this. It's a very sensitive scientific piece of equipment."

Laura finished the de-particlizing and placed the gun down. The onions didn't disappear. "I'm going to run this out now," she said.

Blake immediately picked up the gun and began wielding it about in all directions. "Blake!" shouted Simon and Alvin at the same time. "That's not a toy. You could do serious damage with that thing."

Blake reluctantly put it down. "Sorry. It looks wicked."

"I'll get you two a couple of lattes to start you off," Simon offered, clearly a little shaken. "Why don't you go out and sit with JJ and Professor Cooper?"

Blake and Alex quickly returned to their stations behind the table. Blake took the chair next to Kenn. He watched as JJ signed her name in record time, made small talk with each fan, and sent them off, visibly elated. And through it all she kept smiling. In fact, the event appeared to be energizing her.

Kenn must have noticed the same thing because he leaned over to Blake and said, "She appears to love doing this."

Blake nodded. "It's probably the ultimate honor for an author. To know that readers enjoyed your creation."

Kenn nodded as if he were considering the comment.

Blake felt Alex tug at his sleeve. "Look how close the two of them are sitting. We should be home in no time at all."

Chapter 26

"Ahem. Are you too busy to stop for a moment?" Kenn stood at the doorway of JJ's office, hands in his pocket, rocking on the balls of his feet. She was behind the desk studying her conspiracy book.

"Never for my partner in conspiracy, I mean teaching." JJ smiled up at him. A warm flush engulfed her body. *Yeah, it's good to see him.*

"Come on in and sit down." She closed the book, leaning back in her chair, putting her hands behind her head. He readily stepped in and sat in one of the receiving chairs in front of her desk.

Their team-taught class was progressing better than she could have predicted, especially considering her original obstinate opposition to it.

She was surprised to discover she personally enjoyed his company. While it was a welcomed development, it frightened her as well. She had already acknowledged to herself sexual feelings for him. And now she discovered she liked him as a person. That opened up a whole other can of worms in her book. Sexual feelings she could easily discount. She chalked that one up to hormones. But to enjoy him as a person? Now there was a deadly combination.

"Look what I snagged," he said, as he waved two tickets in the air.

She leaned forward in her chair and quirked an

eyebrow. "Tickets to see Elton John and Billy Joel in concert. On the same stage at the same time?"

"No."

"Tickets to see Paul McCartney, then?" she teased.

"Not quite. But there is some form of music involved."

"Okay, I give. What are the tickets for?"

"This Saturday's football game against Ohio College at Defiance."

She picked up a set of tickets from her desk. "Do they look anything like these?"

They laughed. Every instructor at the university received a minimum of two tickets with the instructions to attend as if their tenured professional life depended on it.

"It comes with the territory, doesn't it?" Kenn asked. "Even though you have tickets of your own, and at the chance you may have already asked the man of your dreams to go with you, I'm going to stick my neck out..." Kenn paused, pursing his lips.

Then he asked with what seemed like the speed of a tommy gun in one single breath, "Would you be kind enough to accompany me to the football game Saturday afternoon?" He released a long and slow exhale.

He looked into her eyes then ran his hand through his hair. "Of course, if you already have plans for the game..."

The whole scenario shot chills up and down her spine. How could she possibly say no to such a wonderful man?

"I'd be honored to go," she said quickly.

His rigid body relaxed some. "Great. Is it okay if I pick you up at one? I know the game doesn't start until two, but I want to give us enough time to fight the crowd."

She laughed. "Are we talking about the same football game? The team I thought we were going to watch hasn't won a game in five years. What makes you think there's going to be a crowd?"

"A rich alumnus donated a jumbotron screen TV for the stadium. This game is the first time it's getting used. And it's being advertised with a tease to pan through the stands to show the fans close up and personal."

"It just might be more interesting than the game itself." She furrowed her brow and asked, "Who would waste money on a losing team with such an extravagant purchase?"

"A former member of the football team."

****

JJ had only been home twenty minutes when she heard Alex and Blake enter the house.

"Did you see the look on Craig's face?" Alex asked.

"I did, indeed. It was priceless."

"JJ, we're home."

"Out here on the front porch," she answered. She had a scrapbook of photos from her marriage to Geoff on her lap. She smiled at them as they rambled on about the events of their day.

Alex was in the middle of telling her about her psychology class when she stopped in mid-sentence. "Something wrong, JJ?"

Without saying a word, Blake rose and went into the house.

Maybe I did write some sensitivity into his character, she thought.

"Nothing, really."

"You're looking awfully sad for someone who says nothing's wrong. Of course, something is wrong. Your two uninvited fictional characters have invaded your life. And then there's the dreaded Cooper at school."

She laughed. "The dreaded Cooper is part of it," she confessed, "but not in the way you think." Alex shifted her weight in the patio chair she had eased herself into as JJ was talking.

"You'll be pleased to know that the Dreaded Cooper and I are going to the football game together Saturday."

Alex immediately jumped up, ran over, and hugged her. "That's wonderful, absolutely wonderful. I'm so glad for you two." Then she paused and looked at JJ. "You don't seem happy about it. Still not sure he's got it to be your hero in your personal love story?"

"Actually, quite the opposite. I find that every day I'm more attracted to him. Not only is he sexy, but he's turning into a great friend too. What more can you ask of a man?"

"Exactly," Alex said, straightening her shoulders. "You taught me that. So, what's the…"

Then Alex glanced down at the scrapbook open to JJ's wedding day.

"Feeling guilty? Feeling like you're betraying your late husband's memory?"

Alex had spoken out loud what JJ had feared to. Large tears rolled down her eyes. Memories of all the good times she had with Geoff overwhelmed her. She had pushed the inevitable fights, arguments, and days they would go without speaking in the background. It was all she could do to answer by simply nodding her head.

Quickly, Alex knelt down beside her. "JJ, I know

you didn't write any late husband into my background, so there's a part of me that doesn't have a clue about the pain you're feeling now. And I know I'm only a two-dimensional character from a romance novel."

JJ sniffled and giggled at that comment. "You've become far more than a two-dimensional character, Alex. At least to me. You're a vibrant young woman and an excellent friend."

"I'm going to try to offer you some advice from my limited background, which incidentally includes your previous three books and several other romance novels I've read since I've been in your world." She cleared her throat.

"You deserve to get on with your life. You can't hide forever behind the covers of your books. You can't live forever on the same pages as your characters. Just as we cut loose from you, so to speak, by popping out of our book, you, too, need to poke your head out of your self-imposed book and look around."

"But I feel as if I'm cheating on him, somehow. I know he's gone. But by going out with Kenn, even to an innocent football game, I feel as if I'm demeaning his memory and everything our marriage meant to us."

"I'm betting Geoff loved you very much."

Again, all JJ could do was nod.

"Do you really think he would want you to spend the rest of your life alone? Do you think that he would want you to be miserable all alone like you are?"

"But I was perfectly happy before I met Kenn," she protested. "My life was going along just fine."

"Was it, really? Can you honestly say you enjoyed all the nights you spent alone?"

"Yeah, I can." She became defensive. Then she

thought about the lonely nights. "Well, most of them."

She struggled to control her tears. "You sure ask a lot of questions. And you're beginning to sound like my sister, Nan."

Alex smiled. "Any resemblance between the characters in your book and real people is purely coincidental. Isn't that the disclaimer you give your readers at the beginning of your books? Before I visited you, I believed that legalese malarkey."

Her character paused and her tone turned serious again. "But seriously, these are only questions you've been asking yourself for so long. Remember, while I've gained some limited knowledge on my own, anything that comes from my heart is there because you placed it in there first. I am first and foremost a creation of JJ Spritely."

Then she smiled broadly and added, "And of that, I'm proud."

JJ laughed out loud at that last comment. Alex continued. "My guess is that Geoff wouldn't want you wallowing around here missing him forever. You've done your share of grieving. Now it's time to get on with your life. I know Geoff would agree."

Blake sprinted out quickly offering JJ a box of tissues. JJ and Alex gave him dirty looks. He smiled back at them, seemingly oblivious to their irritation and sprinted back into the house. JJ pulled several tissues at a time out of the box and blew her nose. Then she took two more to wipe the tears from her eyes and cheeks.

"Besides," Alex offered, "it's only a football game. You're making no lifelong commitments by going to a football game. Just go and have a good time."

"But you're praying that more comes of this," JJ

said, with a slight smile. "You're still convinced he's the next love of my life. And you're still hoping we get together so you can go home."

"Well, yeah. But I realize now that those pleadings and maneuverings were pretty selfish on my part. And I apologize. I looked at your situation through a simplistic lens. Life in this world, I've discovered, has more complexity than I imagined."

JJ wasn't sure she believed a word of what Alex had said but appreciated the thought. She carefully considered her next words.

"It's only natural that you're searching for a way home. And honestly, it seems like a logical way to get back home," JJ admitted. "After all, you leaped out of the pages of a romance novel. How else would you view life?"

She rocked back and forth in the rocker. She stared aimlessly across the street. Mr. Higley had just pulled his red truck into his driveway, stopped it at the end of it as he picked up his mail, waved and smiled at her. "Beautiful day, isn't it," he said.

"It most certainly is, Mr. Higley, it's gorgeous."

"The missus and me are celebrating our fiftieth wedding anniversary today."

"Congratulations, Mr. Higley. Send Mrs. Higley my love."

She could only imagine spending half a century with the same man.

Chapter 27

Kenn sat at the Physics Café, alone in a booth, his back against the wall, legs stretched out along the seat. He looked like a man lost in thought, Blake observed. Did he dare interrupt whatever was going through his mind?

"Go ahead and at least ask." Alex nudged him. "All he could say is no. I'll be over here in this booth. There are a couple of girls from the cheerleading squad I want to talk to."

Blake cleared his throat. "Tell me again why I'm doing this."

"Because we have to find out his true intentions toward JJ. If he isn't ready for a serious relationship with her, then we're just setting her up for heartbreak. And I would hate to be responsible for that. But if he does think he could really care for her, then we're steering the couple toward the love of their lives. Oh, God, at least I hope so."

He had never interfered with anyone's life before. Well, not in a serious way. He had to admit that his antics of the last week or so had really interfered with both JJ's and Kenn's life, perhaps in ways that pushed them toward each other a little sooner than they had anticipated. Then he really thought about it. No, if anything, left solely to his influence, the two wouldn't be talking at all.

"Hi, Kenn," he said casually. "May I join you?" It looked as if Kenn had been studying the whipped cream swirls in his cappuccino.

"Blake." Kenn appeared sincerely pleased to see him. "Of course, you can. Sit down. Where's Alex?" Kenn immediately placed his feet on the ground and swung his torso around so he was facing the other side of the booth.

"She's sitting over there," he said, as he pointed in the general direction of Alex, "talking with some cheerleaders. I didn't think I could survive such an intellectual conversation."

"Don't judge a book by its cover," the professor cautioned.

What an appropriate proverb to use, Blake thought. "Oh, I know. Even though Alex has joined that group, she's a very bright woman. I'm in the process of reassessing my stereotypes about cheerleaders."

"I can tell by her remarks in class that she's got quite a mind." Kenn commented that she had an uncanny insight into conspiracy theories. "But then so do you."

"That's because our memories include…" *No, Blake, don't go there. Use your head for once.* How could he tell Kenn that their knowledge came directly from JJ because she developed their characters? No, that wouldn't work at all.

Instead, he went with the more appropriate reply. "We both seemed to have acquired a passion for the subject. Probably because we've been so close to JJ for so long."

"No doubt." Silence followed. Damn. *It's at this point, Kenn's supposed to start pouring his heart out to me. At least, commenting on something.*

"JJ is truly a remarkable woman," Kenn finally offered, much to his relief.

Even as clueless as he could be at times, Blake could feel that this was his cue. So not having the very literal nudging presence of Alex to help him judge his timing, he pushed on, praying he didn't make a mess of everything, as seemed to be his habit.

"JJ mentioned in passing that you and she are going to the game together tomorrow." He paused, worried about how that sounded. "It only came up in the conversation because we asked her to attend to watch our first show." *Smooth recovery, Mr. Teesdale.*

"Yes, we are." Then silence. If JJ liked the silent type, he thought, she certainly hit the mother lode with this one. He raked his fingers through his hair, then struggled to get his hand through the unruly mop. It got stuck in some knotted underbrush. Finally, he got it out. Then he tried to pretend it never happened.

Finally, Kenn spoke again. "Can I ask you a personal question?" *Well, now we're getting somewhere.*

"Of course, Dr. Cooper."

"Was it love at first sight when you met Alex?" That was not quite the question he expected, but Blake saw it as the perfect opening. He was going to make Alex proud of him. He could feel it now.

"It depends on who you ask."

The professor paused with both hands on his cappuccino cup perched nearly at his lips, ready to take another sip. "I'm asking you."

"Yes, it definitely was." Blake told Kenn about the first time he saw Alex's face. She was sitting all alone in a restaurant, drinking a cup of coffee. How he suavely sat down across from her in the booth. How he said the wrong word and she poured hot coffee on his head and walked out.

Coffee spewed from Kenn's mouth, sloshing from the cup as he rocked with waves of laughter. "What did you say to her to tee her off so badly?" he finally asked as he wiped his face and clothes with a napkin.

"Let's just say, I was trying to give her a very sincere compliment. But my use of American slang was a bit rusty back then." He paused then smiled slightly. "If you could imagine that."

Again, Kenn laughed. Then he appeared to turn thoughtful.

"How did you two ever finally fall in love?"

"Persistence on my part," Blake said, hoping Kenn would see the parallel. *That and the fact that JJ wrote it so she'd finally love me.* How lucky I am, he thought. Up until now he hadn't realized that his perfect mate was as close to a match made in heaven as possible.

"How did you know you needed to persist and not give up?"

"That's a tough question. On the one hand if you push too hard you look like a stalker. But if you let her slip from your life, you may never discover another woman quite like her again."

Blake's voice took on a dream-like quality. He pictured the days before he was certain about Alex's love.

Kenn ventured a comment. "It's clearly evident Alex is madly in love with you. You two have such a perfect romance. It's like the pages of a romance novel come to life."

"W-w-what makes you say that?" Blake asked. The analogy unnerved him. He wondered if Kenn suspected he was a fictional character. He immediately dismissed the idea. Nobody expects to encounter fictional characters in real life. He took a deep breath and refocused on his mission.

"You persist as long as you believe you can love her. And in the process, she gives you hints if you observe her keenly enough."

Chapter 28

Kenn took the three steps up JJ's small, neat front porch and glanced at the several pieces of outdoor furniture. As he stood at the door, he realized a jumble of emotions surged through him. Anticipation, that's for sure. Even a bit of sexual excitement at seeing the attractive history professor. But he hadn't expected the twinge of fear.

He found it difficult to extract one feeling from another and, really, he hadn't examined his feelings since his last girlfriend had abruptly dumped him for the older man on a motorcycle.

Much to his surprise, the one emotion he could dig down and discover was his deep caring for JJ. Holy crap, he thought. *What if she really is the one and I do something to screw it up?*

He looked at his watch. Five minutes to one. *Is it too early to ring the bell? I don't want to appear too eager. Certainly don't want her to think I'm pushy.*

He stood there several more minutes, as he looked around the neighborhood. Then he pulled out his cell phone and checked the time. Two minutes till one. He shifted the weight of his body from one leg to another and glanced at the phone again. The third time he checked his phone it was finally one o'clock.

He stuffed his phone in his pocket and at the same time forced all his fears and all other emotions in him down and rang the doorbell. He put on his best smile. When JJ opened the door, his smile not only brightened, but become much more natural.

"I hope I'm not late."

"Right on time. You couldn't have timed it any better if you had stood out there checking the time." She flashed a smile at him.

He had never seen her in casual dress before. She wore a large, oversized sweatshirt that reminded him of the color of grape jelly. The sweatshirt reached down only partially covering her derriere. He noticed her faded jeans fit her well, snug enough to accentuate the curves of her hips.

"Come in for a moment while I get my coat." She ushered him into the living room while she disappeared into a hallway.

As he waited, he scanned the room. It had a cozy feel to it, with a fireplace on one side and large floral prints on the wall above the couch. He was pleased to see her return, in the middle of shrugging her coat on. She picked up her keys off the end table. "All set."

As he drove to the stadium, he realized it was the first time he had been alone with her for any length of time. That thought and the silence in the vehicle unnerved him momentarily. Thankfully, she had the presence of mind to start a topic.

"Have you noticed that Dr. Chare always seems to be lurking in the hallway during our class? I run into him as I enter the classroom and he's there when I leave. What's up with that?"

"I think he's worried we'll kill each other."

She laughed, and he felt the tension had been broken. For the rest of the short ride, he was more at ease making conversation.

****

"Wow, there really is a lot of traffic going into the

stadium," JJ commented, as they pulled into its parking lot. "Do you think they're all coming to see the big-screen TV?"

"Undoubtedly. Ohio State football we're not. You know what I'm saying?"

She exited the SUV and met up with Kenn at the back of the vehicle. As they made their way toward the ticket gate, she found herself being jostled by the eagerness of so many people heading in. One man, in particular, bumped into her and knocked her off balance. The force of the bump knocked her into Kenn.

"You okay?" he asked as he immediately placed an arm around her shoulder. Her heart skipped a beat.

"I'm good." She glanced up at his deep brown eyes. "Thanks."

He kept his arm in place as they got through the ticket gate, and she made no effort to protest the situation.

They sidled themselves to the middle of the third row of bleachers along the thirty-yard line, excusing themselves as they walked over the feet of those already seated.

"I want to make sure I can see Alex and Blake clearly without some tall person's head in the way."

She realized she felt an unexpected sense of parental pride at her characters' accomplishments and couldn't wait to see them perform.

He quirked an eyebrow. "You do know that means my head will now block some other short person's view?"

She shrugged. "Better them than me," she said as she sat down. "You're obviously not familiar with the Zen of short people: come early; sit close."

"Professors, it's good to see you." She and Kenn turned at the same time to see Dr. Chare and Deb Dilley behind them.

"Why, Dr. Chare," she said, her eyes wide, "I don't think I've ever seen you in anything but a suit." The chairman wore a bright purple sweatshirt with UNO emblazoned on the chest in lime green. She thought the color scheme looked ridiculous on the students. On him it looked atrocious.

"Normally, I wouldn't wear these colors, you understand."

"Completely," Kenn said. "I wonder who came up with this combination?"

"I heard we have the class of 1970 to thank for this psychedelic combination," JJ said.

"Did somebody have a bad acid trip and took the rest of the school with them?" Kenn joked.

JJ found Deb uncharacteristically quiet throughout all this, but she did give her what could only be described as a sly smile. *Oh, no, she's going tell the entire university that Kenn and I were at the game together.*

The marching band began to play, and she and Kenn quickly turned around to face the field. The band, accompanied by the men's pep squad and cheerleaders had just started their traditional warm up act to get the crowd pumped about the game.

Blake, in the costume of Ulysses Uno, led the pep squad in the cheers as the cheerleaders joined in dancing and waving their purple and green pom poms.

The spectators yelled wildly and cheered when the jumbotron captured the images of the fighting finger parading around.

"Is Blake marching or toddling?" she asked, as she

studied him on the TV. "He looks like a child just learning to walk."

Kenn shook his. "When do you suppose we'll get a real mascot?"

"Don't hold your breath. This one has a name now. You know how hard it is to give up a stray cat once you've named him. UNO may never get rid of this mascot now."

After a few moments, the pep squad and cheerleaders yielded the field to the teams and the kickoff signaled the start of the game. She had never been a fan of the game and knew little about it, but she cheered at what seemed to be all the appropriate places, mostly because she thought it was expected of her.

She noticed, though, that Kenn was serious about his football. He reacted fervently to every play regardless of how unimportant she felt it was. It didn't take long, however, before his zeal rubbed off on her and she, too, became more enthusiastic. At the end of the first quarter, the fighting UNOs had hold of the lead, seven to nothing.

In the excitement of the moment, Kenn kissed her on the top of her head. The action startled her, but it definitely wasn't unpleasant. She enjoyed that small sign of affection more than she cared to admit.

"I know very little about football," she confessed during one of the timeouts. "My knowledge about the sport can be summed up in me knowing which way our team should be running and recognizing a touchdown."

She looked up at him. "I guess I'm not the best football buddy you could have." Kenn wore his black jacket unzipped to reveal a nondescript gray sweatshirt. *Even in that, the man is striking.*

In response to her confession of a lack of football

knowledge, he would occasionally get a bit closer to her and clarify the reason for a penalty or the strategy on the field. Bless his heart, she thought, as he explained something dealing with a fourth down. *He's trying hard to explain. And my mind is thinking more about the breathing he's doing in my ear than the game.*

Chapter 29

JJ nudged Kenn.

"Just look at Alex and Blake," she said. "She's got her arms around those curved fingers and thumb like she's going to dance." Their antics amazed her. That parental pride popped up again. *I'm not used to seeing my characters really come to life.*

"Heck, they are dancing. Is that a polka?"

In a matter of minutes, the jumbotron had them up on the screen. The fans cheered, which prompted the band to do their own interpretation of a polka. In no time at all, it seemed everyone in the stadium was up on their feet singing and moving to the beat.

As the song continued, a cheerleader tapped Alex on the shoulder, indicating she wanted to cut in. Alex theatrically stepped aside. Then another danced with Blake. Every cheerleader, in turn, danced with the mascot, even as the game restarted. The crowd didn't seem to care they had missed several plays.

With all the quick dance movements, Blake apparently had become dizzy inside the finger costume.

As soon as the last cheerleader let go of him, he stumbled in circles briefly before falling flat on his back.

It looked like a giant hand lay palm up in the field. Alex rushed over and removed his knuckle head cover.

She tried to smooth his hair down and carefully helped him to his feet. A crescendo of cheers rose from the stands. He turned to the home bleachers and took a bow, nearly tumbling over. A surge of laughter reignited throughout the stadium. His image flashed on the big screen again.

By the time it was halftime, the other team, Ohio College at Defiance, had tied the score, seven to seven. JJ thought the first half of the game had flown by in what must have been the fastest two quarters in football history. She couldn't tell if it was the thrill of the football game that pumped her with adrenaline or the rush she felt being next to Kenn for so long.

The Ohio College at Defiance marching band stepped out onto the field precisely as the announcer called half time. The band acted as if it had one mind, playing a current popular song.

"They're good," she said, as she watched in amazement at the disciplined performance.

"Yeah. Look at them, they're all marching in perfect time. Not a leg raised too early or too late," Kenn said.

"I swear you can see the creases in their uniforms," JJ commented. Indeed, the blue and white uniforms appeared freshly pressed, fitting each musician as if it were custom made.

The first selection ended, and much to the evident delight of the spectators, the band bowed as one, each of them bending their torsos at the exact same angle. After several seconds, they all returned to their upright positions with the same robotic precision and started the next song.

"I wonder how long they practiced to get that structured," she asked.

"Well, let's just say that they take their school initials seriously."

"What do you mean?"

"Ohio College at Defiance. OCD. Obsessive Compulsive Disorder?"

She laughed and lightly slapped his arm. He wrapped his arm around her and pulled her close. Then, as if having second thoughts, he released his grip and stuffed his hands in his pockets. She savored the all-too-brief moment.

The OCD band finished their portion of the halftime show, took another precise bow, and exited the field with the same panache as they entered.

"And now ladies and gentlemen, we present the University of Northern Ohio Marching Band!" The announcer's deep, professional voice rung out.

A few, long awkward seconds passed. No band.

The voice gave it another try. "Ladies and gentlemen. We're proud to present the University of Northern Ohio Marching Band!"

Still no band appeared, but the clash of symbols, the beating of drums, and a few off-tone unrecognizable instruments echoed through the stadium. Finally, the band stumbled out. Their purple and lime green uniforms were topped by hats with plumes of the same colors wobbling precariously from side to side.

JJ watched nearly stupefied as the band tried to march. She nudged Kenn. "They're having a tough time playing the entire song together, like a band usually does."

"That wouldn't be so bad," Kenn said, grinning, "if those who actually played got the notes right."

No sooner had he spoken, than the woodwinds went musically rogue, each instrument apparently playing their own melody, horribly off key. JJ cringed at the discordant notes. Finally, the brass section drowned them out. Just when all the instruments appeared to be playing together, the cymbalist tripped and his instrument clanged unexpectedly, startling the other members and the crowd.

The announcer introduced the group's finale as if it were some magic trick. "And for your musical enjoyment and delight, the band will perform a popular song while creating Script Ohio."

She moaned and rested her forehead on Kenn's arm. "I see disaster in their future and I'm not even psychic."

The band began to form the capital "O." Okay, so it looked more like a "U." Then they tackled the "H." But the true chaos erupted when the band, in an attempt to create the "I," crisscrossed each other. The hat of the trombonist slipped off his head and covered his eyes. He apparently got disoriented and turned in the opposite direction he should have, and slammed into a fellow trombonist. The slides of their instruments struck each other, got hopelessly entangled, and took them both down.

Sprawled out on the field, there was no way that poor bass drummer could avoid them. He tumbled over them landing smack dab on top of the pair. One of the trombonists was caught under the drum, only his legs visible. In the process of trying to extricate himself, his trombone tore the skin of the drum.

The drummer furiously freed himself from the ugly wreckage, attacked the offending trombonist, and wrapped his hands around his neck. It took two trumpet players, three clarinetists, and a flutist to separate the pair.

When they were finally at a safe distance from each

other the crowd cheered.

"Are they cheering because the fight got broken up or for the original disaster?" JJ asked.

"Hard to tell. Definitely hard to tell."

Hearing the approval of the crowd, the participants of the fight along with those who intervened took a bow.

"What is Blake doing?" she asked. She pointed at him as he waddled out on the sidelines and began to lead the spectators in cheers.

"Apparently an attempt to salvage the moment?" Kenn quirked an eyebrow.

The cheerleaders joined in to prepare the fans for the second half as the band left the field.

"We're definitely not OCD." Kenn spoke into her ear.

****

"I can't believe the Fighting Fingers are so close to winning," JJ said as she and Kenn again jumped to their feet after the team completed an incredibly long pass.

It was late in the fourth quarter and the score was fourteen to seven—with UNO ahead.

"Don't get too excited," Kenn cautioned, "the game isn't over yet." He tapped her arm. "Did you see that kid who just ran down the field?"

"Yeah, what about him?" She turned to look at him. His brown eyes met hers. She sighed.

"That's Justin Lambert."

"Justin? Our Justin from the conspiracy class?"

"Yep. One and the same."

"Yay, Justin!" JJ shouted. Unfortunately, her late cheer echoed through the stadium at an unusually quiet time and sounded louder than she had intended. She tugged at Kenn's sweatshirt and apologized.

"No need to." He smiled down at her, hesitantly placing his arm around her. Surprised, but by no means upset, she sidled a little closer to him, enjoying the moment.

Chapter 30

From the sidelines, Alex ran over to Blake, who was in the final stanzas and antics of a cheer. She pointed to where the two professors were standing.

He took the best hard look he could, considering the combined restraints of his finger costume and the knuckle head cover. He punched his arms out of the holes and placed his arms around the love of his life, pulling her as close as he could—considering the circumstances.

"We're on the right track," she said. "They look great together." Blake's giant fingernail nodded yes. And the fighting finger gave out a big sigh.

At that moment, the buzzer signaled the end of the game. UNO had won its first game in five years with a score of fourteen to seven. Alex and Blake grabbed each other, hopping around on the field like a couple of rabbits. He finally stopped, stripped his knuckle head cover off and planted a long, hard kiss on Alex's lips.

The rest of the cheerleaders and the men's pep squad burst into a grand chorus of "aw." The pair reluctantly parted lips as their friends pointed to the big screen. The moment had been broadcast—up close and personal—to the entire stadium.

The image then switched to another couple blissfully enthralled in a long and passionate kiss—JJ and Kenn. Alex grabbed Blake.

Arms wrapped around one another, lips exploring each other, the kiss was anything but an ordinary aren't-we-glad-UNO-won peck on the lips. No, their smoldering passion sparked into longing and hunger quickly. It was plain enough. Especially to the two veterans of romance pages. If the game's outcome ignited the moment of passion, that initial kindling was soon fanned as the embers caught fire with this long, indulgent kiss.

"The moment looks so passionate on the big screen." Alex pointed to the jumbotron. She whispered to Blake, "Look at that, will you. JJ's been holding out on us, in those pages she's been writing. If she's got that much passion in her, so do we." She paused and gave Blake a long look from head to toe. "Wait till I get you home tonight." He got as close as he could to her again considering the shape of the mascot's outfit, wrapped his arms partially around her, kissed her hair delicately, and just stood there for a moment.

****

The professors slowly became aware that a collective "aw" filled the stadium, intruding on the moment. JJ was the first to open her eyes and stole a glance around. In a spurt, she pushed herself away from Kenn. His grip on her was strong and he wasn't ready to release her, so she couldn't put much distance between them.

Her eyes involuntarily followed what everyone else was watching—the jumbotron. The images of her and Ken stood, larger than life, featured in the middle of the screen as entertainment for the rest of the fans.

Absolutely humiliated, totally confused, her cheeks hot with humiliation, she wished there was a rock to crawl under. The best she could find, though, was Kenn's jacket. She raised one side up and stuck her head in it, like an ostrich sticks his head in the sand. Kenn held her with both arms tightly wrapped around her small frame.

The big screen TV captured this as well. The crowd laughed, then cheered, then applauded.

A small, muffled voice from within his shirt pleaded, "Take me home now…please."

Chapter 31

The ride from the stadium to JJ's home was excruciatingly silent. JJ sat, hands wrapped around her body, staring out the windshield.

"I think I owe you—" he began.

"Don't. Say. A. Word." She gave him a look that he knew reinforced the words. He didn't dare speak. What an ass I truly am, he thought, as he decided to keep his view on the road and his mouth shut. *The last thing I need is to get into an accident while I'm attempting to explain myself. She really would never talk to me again.*

He sighed deeply as he stopped for a traffic light and noticed that it did cause her to glance over at him. He couldn't even imagine what was going through her mind. On second thought, oh yes, he could. It was official. He had no hope of ever getting any closer to her. Damn it.

Mercifully, he finally pulled into her driveway. Even before the car fully stopped, she had begun to open the door. He worried she would accuse him of pushing her out of a moving vehicle.

Before she exited, she did nod over to him and whisper a thank you. He nodded in return. He was at a loss of what to say to her. He watched as she hurried up the driveway to the back of her house, where she disappeared from his sight.

He lingered a few moments in the driveway. He tried to think of a way to follow her to apologize that didn't seem desperate or stalker-like. He eventually gave up on the idea. He sighed as he put the car in reverse, placed his left arm over his seat, and backed out. As he pulled onto the roadway, he stared at the house as if the action would bring JJ running to the window to…well, what he had no idea.

He drove toward home, but suddenly decided he didn't want to sit alone sulking, so he made a quick right turn and headed for the Physics Café. If he was going to sulk, he would do it around joyous people. He could only imagine the celebration taking place there. After all, for everyone else at the University of Northern Ohio, it was indeed a remarkably joyful day.

The café was crowded with noisy, enthusiastic students. It was a fluke Kenn found an empty booth after he placed his order and took his element placard.

Or was it a fluke?

He felt the eyes of German physicist Werner Heisenberg on him as he looked up and saw the man's Uncertainty Principle written out next to his portrait. He didn't understand a single symbol of the equation, but he knew the word "uncertainty" summed up his current situation all too well.

Not only the relationship he had hoped to have with JJ was uncertain, but his ill-timed action even put his professional rapport with the wonderful woman in jeopardy.

His element number was called, 10Ne, and he picked up his Higgs-Boson Bison Burger and side of Onion String Theory. He had just bit into his burger when Dr. Chare and Deb came up to him.

"Where's JJ? Why isn't she with you?" Deb flashed him a smile and then said sweetly, "You two seemed so close at the game."

"Professor, may we sit with you?" Chare asked. Kenn was off the hook for answering Deb, at least for the moment. He knew, though, she wouldn't drop the conversation that easily. "It seems as if all the other accommodations are full. It's not every day the student body receives an opportunity to celebrate a Fighting Fingers victory."

It was against his better judgment, but he really had no recourse. He couldn't very well refuse his boss. Of course, Deb Dilley was another matter. "Please, I wouldn't have it any other way."

"Thank you." It had seemed they had already passed by him once on the way to the register, since the man had the periodic element of 2He.

He and Chare made small talk, which mostly centered on other professors, until his number was called. Chare excused himself.

Deb didn't waste any time returning to the topic of JJ in his absence. *She must have been sitting on pins and needles waiting for the chair to leave.*

"So, where is JJ? I would have thought she would be with you celebrating the big win." She raised her eyebrows as she reached for her Pomegranate Proton Smoothie.

Kenn shifted his weight as he tried to think of a noncommittal comment. "She wanted to go home." *Immediately.*

"That's a shame. You two looked like you were getting along so well." She paused. "The jumbotron really caught you in a close moment."

Just then, Chare came back with the food. He settled in and gave Deb her Chernobyl Chicken Meltdown and

143

Feynman Fries. He picked up his Philadelphia Experiment Cheesesteak. He went to take a bite, but hesitated.

"Do I note a bit of tension at the table since I left?" Chare turned to eye Deb. "Don't tell me you brought up Kenn and JJ's experience with the jumbotron?"

He didn't think anyone could make Deb feel remorseful. But he was wrong. Deb looked like a small child getting reprimanded for acting out in public.

Chare put his sandwich down and turned his attention to Kenn. "Son, it seems to me that you and JJ may have something special that goes beyond a professional affinity." He paused, as if he were choosing his words carefully.

"That's rare in this day. JJ has experienced more loss than any young woman should in her life. I do believe she feels something special for you. Just give her time. All she needs is a little time."

He took a bite of his sandwich. "But you didn't hear that from me."

Chapter 32

"Did you see what I did? Why, of course, you did. It was broadcast on international TV, for crying out loud. The entire world saw it."

JJ slammed her purse on the dining room table, then dragged herself to the living room where she collapsed on the couch slouching with her legs extended.

"You kissed a man, that's all," Alex said as she sat on the arm of the chair next to her.

"And wow, did you kiss him good," Blake added, standing in the middle of the living room, still in the palm part of his mascot's uniform.

"Blake." Alex glared at him.

"But truthfully," she said as she turned her attention back to her creator, "I missed it. I was busy with the man of my dreams."

Even in her state of desperation, JJ couldn't help but notice that Blake, with his hair still an unmanageable mess from his character's outfit, beamed with pride.

"I didn't kiss just any man"—she ran her hand through her hair and held it for a moment—"but Kennedy King Cooper." She released her hand from her head and allowed her hair to fall to one side. "How could I let myself do that?"

"Perhaps because you're finally allowing yourself to recognize those feelings you have for him?" Alex

145

ventured.

"Even if I do, I can't show them. We work together."

"That's just a flimsy excuse," Blake said. "You know full well that's not the reason you're flummoxed like you are."

"I am not flummoxed." JJ's high-pitched voice startled her. Then she looked at Alex and asked out loud, "Flummoxed? Where did you get that word?"

"From our book. Chapter six, to be exact. When Alex's old love comes to town and her feelings are torn between him and me. She was flummoxed."

The author squinted her eyes, trying to switch gears thinking back to the novel.

"I do believe you're right, Blake. She was flummoxed, wasn't she?"

"People, let's focus here. The issue at hand is not my flummoxing," Alex said, attempting to re-direct the conversation back to JJ. "Right now, we're discussing JJ's apparent horror at actually kissing a man. That's much more interesting to talk about."

"No, it definitely is not," JJ said. She paused a beat before adding, "More importantly, it's not a good position to be in, professionally speaking." She kicked off her shoes, re-positioned herself, then brought her feet up on the couch and tucked them underneath her.

"To bloody hell with professionally speaking," Blake spewed out. "In the short time we've been observing you from the pages of your own world, so to speak, you have not allowed yourself one moment of pure pleasure, doing something just for yourself. You have to be dragged out of the house to actually interact with real people on any regularity. Face it, you were afraid of stepping out of your snug, secure cocoon. The truth of the matter is you're not really living."

Alex bolted upright from the arm of the chair. "Why Blake Teesdale, I didn't know you had such keen powers of observation when it comes to reading people. I'm not only impressed, I'm extremely proud of you."

She strode up to him, leaned over the palm of his costume, and kissed him on the cheek.

Blake not only beamed, he blushed. "So, let's get down to the nitty gritty as they say. What exactly do you think is the cause of your flummoxed state?"

When his question was met with a stare, Alex said, "Let's phrase it this way. What were you feeling when you kissed Kenn?"

"Aside from an incredible sexual urge to disrobe him right in the stadium," he suggested.

"Blake!" JJ and Alex both shouted at him.

He placed a hand on his hip. "You probably were feeling it. I know I was when kissing Alex in that scene in chapter seven…"

"Blake!"

"Now, back to the question at hand." Alex tried to refocus the conversation again. "I know this sounds personal. But if you can't talk to us, JJ, who can you talk to?"

A weak smile crossed her mouth. Certainly, these two were closer to her than even her own sister. "Well, the thought momentarily did cross my mind of dragging him behind the stadium…"

"La, la, la," Blake said, as he covered his ears. Alex laughed and JJ joined in.

"You were the one who brought up the subject," his girlfriend said.

JJ continued. "It was an exciting feeling, that's for

sure. And if you want to know the truth, it felt quite liberating."

Alex sat down next to her on the couch and gave her what could only be described as a motherly look. "Great. So, what's the problem?"

She unfolded her legs and stood. She sighed deeply, then paced. "The truth is," she said quietly. "I'm scared. I haven't felt like this in ages. And, well," she paused and turned to look at Alex. "I'm concerned I'm setting myself up for a real heartbreak here. Unlike your love story, mine might not end in a happily-ever-after. I might never find another Geoff St. Clair. Then what do I do?"

"You pick yourself up, dust yourself off, and start all over again," sang Blake.

JJ groaned.

"Okay, so in a song it sounds, well, Pollyannaish," Blake defended himself. "But isn't that exactly how you go through life? You encounter the good and the bad. The pleasant and the unpleasant. But you just keep going. You cherish the good and learn from the mistakes and the misfortunes. You certainly don't cut yourself off from the world."

She stopped pacing, turned toward Blake, hands on hips. "Do you really think that's what I've been doing?"

The silence echoed throughout the room.

"Aha!" Blake hurriedly wiggled out of his mascot costume and tossed it on the recliner.

"I know how to show your current non-relationship with Professor Cooper." His hair flounced as he dashed into the kitchen. "Sit down on the couch. I'm sure you'll find relevance in this analogy."

She crossed the room and sat next to Alex. She heard the refrigerator door open, then what sounded like Blake rummaging through it. What in the world? She glanced at Alex, who appeared just as perplexed. Alex smiled meekly and shrugged.

He returned, his hair still a barometer of his enthusiasm. He pulled a TV tray from between the side of the couch and the wall and set it up squarely in front of the couch. It reminded her of a stage. He dropped his props on it—four slices of cheese, two slices of bread, and a roll of wax paper.

Then he politely excused himself, as he trotted to the linen closet in the hallway. He came back with her iron. He momentarily looked around for an electrical outlet, then smiled broadly when he found it. He plugged in the iron and set it on the tray. Alex nudged her. "Doesn't he look like a magician preparing for his act."

She nodded. "Maybe you should go up there and be his beautiful assistant."

"Not me. I'm not sure what he's up to. It could be dangerous."

Blake cleared his throat. "I heard that," he said. He shifted his weight and began his presentation.

"My dear ladies." He bowed low at the waist.

"He looks so professional," Alex whispered. JJ thought otherwise, with the man's hair bouncing everywhere, but she kept her comment to herself.

He picked up a slice of cheese wrapped in cellophane in his right hand. "Allow me to show you why, at this point in time, JJ Spritely…" He nodded at the object, which gave the impression it represented her. "…and Professor Kennedy King Cooper…" He picked up another slice of cheese and held it high.

It was now clear to her, the other cheese slice was supposed to be Kenn. He paused, raised his eyebrows, and took a deep breath. She waited.

"…are not finding true romance and lasting love at this time."

She bit her lip and ran a hand through her hair. Alex shifted her weight on the couch. It was anyone's guess where this display of dairy products was going.

"The problem? The obvious," Blake said, as he waved both slices. "Each hermetically sealed. Not allowing the other inside to reach their feelings." He paused and eyed her. Her gut told her this act was headed for disaster.

"But even if these two self-protected people were to unwrap their cellophane," he said, carefully taking the wrapper off one slice, then the other. "We'd discover that they aren't sincerely showing the other who they really are. Right now, they're poor imitations of real cheese. They are, as the package warns you, processed cheese food products."

He continued. "Now let's explore the possibilities of what these two could be experiencing." He paused a beat and flashed her a smile. She grew more worried.

"First, they could voluntarily shed the protective wrapper—" he theatrically picked up a slice of real deli cheese "—allowing the other to see them. That, by the way, is the basis of any good friendship." He nodded toward JJ.

"Now, in this situation we have two real slices of cheese—I mean people—who are starting their relationship on the right foot." He smiled as if he were quite pleased with the progress of his presentation.

"But that's not all." He carefully placed the two slices of real cheese together. "Notice how much closer they are. Now let's just go one step farther." He picked up one of the slices of bread. "We place the two of them together. We allow these two to spend some time alone." Blake carefully placed the two slices together on the bread. He then placed the second slice on top of the cheese. He held the sandwich high.

He put the sandwich on the tray, and picked up the roll of wax paper, tore off a sheet long enough to cover it, and then picked up the iron. "And we allow events to heat up a bit."

He licked his index finger, touching it to the hot surface of the iron. Immediately, he flinched. "Ouch. Definitely hot enough." Then he ironed the sandwich and hummed for several seconds. JJ glanced at Alex, then shifted her weight.

After what he apparently considered a sufficient amount of time, Blake set the iron aside, picked up the sandwich, and tore it open.

Gooey, melted cheese oozed from the two halves. "And so you see," he said as if he were a science professor demonstrating an experiment for his students, "the two previously separate slices of cheese are now living happily ever after as one. That, ladies, is the ultimate secret to a successful relationship." He ceremoniously bowed.

Alex sprang from her seat, applauding. "Bravo! Bravo!" She dashed to his side and gave him a hug and a kiss. "You're awesome, hon!"

JJ just sat on the couch, stunned, mouth hanging open in amazement. "I can't believe you've just reduced my love life to a grilled cheese sandwich."

She jumped up, ran to her bedroom, and slammed the door.

Chapter 33

JJ took a deep breath as she climbed the stairs leading to the entrance of Mundain Hall, the building that housed the history department. One of the oldest structures on campus, it was named for a now long-gone beloved history professor. At one time it was a stately reminder of the past. Now it was merely old.

"Monday morning," she muttered, "and a chance to put Saturday's horrendous incident behind me."

As she walked down the hall, she noticed two coeds pointing at her office door, giggling. *What in the world? What are they looking at?* Apparently hearing her approach, one of them looked her way.

"Oh, my God," JJ heard one of them say, as she nudged the other, "there she is now. Let's get out of here." The other student gave her a quick glance as if to confirm her friend's observation, they both giggled, and then hurried down the hall.

Click. Click. Click. The accelerated rate of her heels indicated her growing concern of what could possibly be on the door. When she finally saw the large, clear, crisp, color image plastered on her door, her knees turned to rubber and she dropped her messenger bag.

"I don't believe this. This can't be happening to me." A student photographer had captured the jumbotron image of her and Kenn in their passionate kiss. The photo was large and thanks to some editor at the UNO's student newspaper, *The Daily Digit,* was now on the front page and distributed campus-wide. *So much for putting the horrendous incident behind me.*

Above the photo was a headline: *Professors In Love.* Below the photo was a brief explanation: *History professors, Kennedy King Cooper and J. Jordan St. Clair share an intimate moment in front of the entire UNO stadium as the Fighting Fingers win their first football game in five years (See the Sports Page for more details on the game.).*

"Why me?" The words came out as a whimper. It was really all the energy she could expend at the moment. Her whole world was unraveling at a most alarmingly brisk rate. She sighed heavily and leaned her head on the door. Her initial reaction was to hit her head against it, and, in fact, she did raise it. But she stopped just short of the fulfilling the action.

"With my luck," she sighed, "I'd break the window. And the school newspaper would have a field day with that."

Instead, she settled for ripping the page from the door. She dragged herself into her office and immediately closed the door behind her. All she wanted was a few minutes alone to pull herself together before she had to face her class.

And Kenn. God, she had to look Kenn in the face. She tossed the page in the trash can and unceremoniously dumped her messenger bag on a chair.

It wasn't until she walked around to sit down that she noticed them. The unexpected appearance of a thing of beauty made her smile, despite her gloomy mood. She tilted her head and squinted one eye, just to make sure she was seeing what she thought she was seeing. A crystal vase of bright yellow roses sat in the middle of her cluttered desk.

She pulled the card stuck in the middle of the arrangement and opened it. It contained only two words: *I'm sorry.* She laughed to herself. Even though the sender hadn't signed it, she knew who it came from.

"I am, you know." She knew the voice even before she looked in the direction of it. She pivoted to face Kenn.

"I lost control," he said, "I was totally out of line."

She watched in fascination as Kenn closed his eyes tightly, winced, and appeared to tense every muscle in his body. His arms quickly and instinctively protected his face, and he raised his left knee—as if he expected to be kicked in the lower part of his body.

"Go ahead," he said. "I'm ready for it."

She moved swiftly out from behind her desk to stand directly in front of him.

"What are you doing?"

"Preparing myself for the lashing you're about to unleash on me."

"What?"

"You know, you're going to tell me I'm a pompous ass—no wait—make that an audacious pompous ass, a sexist elitist, and who knows what else. I'm ready for it."

"Now, why would I do that?" She dropped the card and placed her hands on her hips.

Not changing his stance one bit but beginning to totter a little unsteadily, he answered, "Because you did it when I first met you at the bookstore, then again at the café, and you were especially effective at your sister's. And this is a much larger transgression."

He paused. "Have you seen the front page of *The*

Daily Digit yet?" He whispered the question and moved his hand slightly as if making sure his eyes were completely covered.

"Yes, as a matter of fact, the damned thing was taped to my door." She took several steps to her trash can, pulled it out, and tried to smooth the page out. "See?"

She watched with curiosity as he slowly moved the two fingers that covered his eyes. He nodded quickly, then put his fingers back in place. Then out of seemingly nowhere, she laughed. The robustness of its sound startled even her. But she couldn't stop.

"What's so funny?" He again deliberately moved his fingers.

"You are." Trying to catch her breath, she continued. "You…look…you look like a giant flamingo practicing tai chi."

Allowing his body to relax, he dropped his arms and put his leg down.

"And really, this whole situation is funny. Hilarious, really," she said between her now uncontrollable laughter.

The pieces of the puzzle of the last couple of weeks were finally falling into place for her. The full effects of Saturday's incident, and the time the two of them had spent teaching and visiting in each other's offices struck her. But what really grabbed her attention was her uncontrollable laughter. It had felt good…extremely good.

"Damn it," she finally said out loud, massaging her forehead with her hand. Kenn returned to his flamingo-performing-tai-chi posture.

"I really am sorry," he whispered.

"Well, you shouldn't be," she murmured. "I just had an epiphany. And I decided I'm not sorry."

He raised an eyebrow. "Who are you, and what did you do with JJ Spritely?" he asked. "Are you some space alien who took her form? Really, this is not the JJ Spritely I know."

"I'll admit it," she began, "I was appalled at first. But just now, I realized I hadn't laughed like that in years. How sad is that? And that kiss we shared? If you didn't notice, I did little to discourage you. I haven't felt that, well, for a long, long time. My sister, and my characters—I mean my cousins—were right."

She deliberately measured her words, like a metronome in slow motion. "I've been hiding in the pages of my books. And now, I'm finally taking a step outside of them and I'm beginning to live in the real world."

Again, he relaxed his stance. "Glad I could be of assistance."

His smile transformed his entire appearance. He looked boyish, almost roguish.

They approached each other slowly, locking eyes. As she got closer to him, she caught a glimpse of the beautiful yellow roses on her desk. She felt his sensual energy. She wasn't sure how any of this would end, but she was certain of one thing: Kenn was trying hard. And that was all she really needed to know.

Before she realized it, she melted into his arms, his lips tightly engaged with hers. Her fingers raked his hair, her nails lightly digging into his scalp. She slowly moved her hands lower, pulling him closer to her.

She felt the pleasure of the kiss and his breath giving her new life, allowing her to be reborn and start again, allowing her to savor the sensual pleasures of his body.

"Wait," she said through the kiss. But he didn't, or couldn't, stop. So, she gently maneuvered the two of them to the door. With her back facing it and using one foot, pushed it shut.

"Lock it," she requested. He wordlessly replied with the request, deftly and swiftly pushing the knob to the locked position.

Seconds later there was a knock at the door. They ignored it.

Bam! Bam!

"Go away." she instructed. She heard the conversation on the other side.

"We just wanted to give you some copies of today's *Daily Digit.*" It was Alex. "We'll just leave them here at the door. Talk to you later."

"Thank you," she said.

"What did she say?" It was Blake's voice.

"She told us to go away." She heard the sound of clicking heels and the protests of Blake.

"But I don't understand what just happened. How did you understand any of that?"

"Do I really have to spell it out for you?" She heard the sound of Blake's tennis shoes being dragged along the wooden floor echoed in the hallway.

"Class starts soon," Kenn said.

Slowly, reluctantly, he released his grip on her.

He stared down at her as he held her at arm's length. "What a glorious epiphany you experienced, Professor St. Clair. Thank you for sharing it with me."

She sighed. "I'm not sure where this is ultimately headed. And I'm not sure how far I'm capable of going. And I'm definitely not very confident how fast I can go there," she said.

She could tell by the creases around his eyes that he was totally amused. "What's so funny?"

"You. You don't know where you're going or how fast you can get there…wherever it is you might be going."

"Despite my confusion, Professor Cooper, there is one thing I'm certain of. I'd really love it if you would go with me. It might turn out to be an interesting trip." She paused as she soaked in his brown eyes.

"Right now, though," she said, with a reluctance that even surprised her, "we need to head straight to the classroom."

Chapter 34

Blake craned his head out the classroom door. "They're almost here. Get ready."

He and Alex had planned this moment the night before, when Alex had received a text with a heads up that the photo would appear on the front page. She had wanted to do something special to celebrate the moment. Blake took the ball from there.

He hurriedly sprinted back to his seat, his hair bouncing all the way. Alex gave him a quick kiss on the cheek.

JJ and Kenn walked into the room.

The students erupted. "Way to go!" "History professors rock." "History profs do it better!"

In addition to a variety of imaginative slogans, many of the students whistled and cheered. They ended their antics with a standing ovation. Neither professor looked appreciative. The room fell silent for a moment.

"Look behind you," a student cried out, breaking the painful silence. The pair turned at the same instant. Copies of the front page of *The Daily Digit* covered every inch of the chalk board.

"I'll get these down right now." Kenn took deliberate steps toward the wall. Alex began to sob, and Blake wrapped an arm around her. "It's all right, love."

"Blake Teesdale. Come help me with these. Now." The intensity of Kenn's words brought Blake to his feet immediately and he scrambled to get to the front of the classroom, his hair wildly bouncing as he sprinted forward.

After the pages had been torn down, Blake meekly walked back to his seat. Alex instantly kissed him. "I thought it was a good idea, if that helps."

Blake smiled and nodded. "Regardless," he said, "I do believe we may be in trouble with JJ tonight."

He and Alex were unusually silent through the rest of the hour.

****

JJ unlocked the back door, and as she walked through the kitchen, she casually dropped her purse and messenger bag on the table.

She padded into the living room, dropped down on the couch, and kicked off her shoes. And she waited.

It didn't take long. She knew it wouldn't. After all, she knew their schedules well. Alex and Blake entered quietly, speaking to each other in whispers. She figured they knew what was in store for them when they got home. It sounded as if they tip-toed through the kitchen and attempted to glide through to the bedroom without being detected.

"Wait one minute," she said. The pair froze at the entrance of the hallway between the kitchen and the dining room.

"Aren't you going to stop to talk?"

"Lots of homework tonight," Alex offered.

"Got to work on that essay for your class," Blake said. "And then we have to prepare for the next event for the spontaneous text marketing business for the Physics Café. Busy. Busy. Busy."

"You have time for this," she said, rising to her feet.

She hoped that by standing up it made her look more authoritative despite her diminutive stature.

"Did you two have any hand in the orchestrating the 'pep rally of love' today in class?"

Blake nervously ran a hand through his hair and stared down at his shoes like a little boy caught filching cookies from the cookie jar. Alex shuffled her pack back from one shoulder to the other. Neither one said a word. Neither of them would meet her eyes.

"I thought so. Please don't ever do that again," she said, as she sat back down.

Blake's gaze immediately shot up. "No lecture?"

Alex walked into the living room and dropped her backpack on the chair. She glanced at JJ sideways, as if perhaps the worst was still to come. "No reminder of how we're meddling in your personal affairs?"

"Not this time."

They relaxed, and faint smiles crept over their faces. Blake walked into the living room and sat on the edge of the couch. Alex dropped next to him, placing her hand on his thigh. His face brightened.

"This doesn't mean I'm not furious," she said. "And totally embarrassed. But I'm not going to dwell on it any longer."

Blake stood up to go. "I just have one question," he said. Alex rolled her eyes.

JJ took in a deep breath. Then she exhaled. "What?"

"Just what was happening in your office when we knocked this morning? I didn't understand a word of what you were—"

"Blake!" The women shouted. Alex snatched his hand and dragged him off toward the bedroom. Before they got too far, JJ called for Alex.

"Thank you, by the way," she said. "Our talk over the weekend put a lot of issues in focus."

Alex smiled. She couldn't help but add in a small whisper, "We're even going out on our first date this weekend."

Alex jumped up and down like a high school girl. "I'm so glad for you." She bent down and gave her a quick hug before she ran off to her bedroom.

Chapter 35

It was a quiet Italian restaurant. The perfect setting, JJ thought, for their first formal date. She felt the warmth of Kenn's hand on her back as he deftly guided her into the small but cozy foyer. Artificial trees of some unknown variety separated the foyer and part of the dining room, while the soft lighting provided the perfect ambiance against the wine-red carpeting and walls. It had been years since she had been on a date. Fear. Anticipation. Excitement. Emotions cascaded around her, none of them staying long enough to recognize.

"I hope you like this place. I asked among the faculty members, and they all agreed *Mario and Luigi's* was the best Italian restaurant in town." Kenn paused. "Okay, it's the *only* Italian restaurant in town."

As they made their way through the foyer, they reached the maître d' looking quite proper and imposing. Kenn said they had a reservation. The maître d' looked at them, glaring critically over his reading glasses as he purposely walked to his podium.

He took his eyes off them for only a second to study the seating chart. Staring through his reading glasses precariously balanced on the end of his eagle-like nose, he fingered the reservation book. His actions, she thought, were birdlike and reminded her of a hawk.

The maître d' looked sharply in their direction, then, much to her surprise, forced a bright smile. It seemed as if a bolt of energy shot through his body as he retrieved two menus from the side of the podium and ushered them to their seats.

"Do you know him?"

She shook her head. "I've never been in this restaurant before."

"Perhaps he's a fan."

"A closet conspirator. How exciting."

"I was thinking more in lines of a closet romantic."

Kenn assisted JJ with her chair then sat down. The maître d' again smiled broadly. It appeared it was not something that he was used to doing nor did it come easily to him. He hurriedly left.

Fairly quickly a waiter stood before them with a bottle of wine. Just as she was about to say she didn't think she wanted a glass, he explained it was a present from the management. He then went through all the formal rituals associated with opening the bottle at the table, allowing each of them to taste it.

He filled the glasses, announced the specials for the day, and promised he'd be back in a few moments to take their orders.

"You seem to be very important around here, JJ."

"I'm not sure why. I have a hard time believing this is because of me. Are we the ten-thousandth customer or something?"

She no sooner finished asking her question when two short, rather pudgy, nearly roly-poly men in formal black tuxedoes appeared in front of them.

"Hello. Hello," they said together.

"My name is Mario," said the one and nodded.

"And I'm Luigi." The other man nodded as well.

Together they said, "Welcome to *Mario and Luigi's*

Italian Bistro."

"Thank you," Kenn said, but they weren't talking to him, they were talking to JJ. He leaned over and said, "This place should be named Bird Land. These guys look just like penguins."

The two of them did look like identical twins. Both were about the same height, not any taller than five feet. Both wore their hair in the classic bowl cut with bangs so far down they merged with their thick eyebrows. And both sported a healthy, thick mustache.

"Don't be silly," she whispered. "Penguins don't have mustaches."

"We are so honored to have you here tonight," Mario said.

"Indeed, we are honored to have you here tonight," repeated Luigi, adding, "We hope you find everything to your satisfaction."

Feeling a bit uncomfortable because the pair hadn't yet taken their eyes off of her, she managed a nervous smile and answered. "I'm quite sure we will. This is the first time I've ever been here."

"Oh yes, we know," said Mario. *Or was that Luigi?*

"But we're hoping it won't be the last," the other added. "If you need anything at all, Ms. Yaki, you just ask your server. He's the best we have. And if that doesn't satisfy you, then you request us." Mario winked and they toddled away.

She and Kenn sat silently for a moment, mouths agape. Kenn spoke first. "He called you Ms. Yaki. Do you know who he thinks you are?"

"Some misplaced Chinese take-out meal?"

"No, he thinks you're the food critic for the *Bell Wyck Tribune*."

"No, he doesn't. He couldn't." She knitted her brow and thought about it for a moment before dismissing the idea. "Absolutely not."

"Her name is Teri Yaki."

"Well, aren't they going to be surprised when there's no review in the paper tomorrow morning?" She laughed. She paused a beat. "They'll be sorry they opened this bottle of wine." She took another sip. "I find this very amusing. Embarrassing, but amusing."

Chapter 36

It was a quiet Italian restaurant. Or at least it was until the two figures, clad in beige trench coats, wide-brimmed hats, and oversized sunglasses stepped in.

They paused briefly in the lobby of *Mario and Luigi's Italian Bistro*. Alex lifted her sunglasses and swiftly, using exaggerated moves, scanned the layout. Taking several steps forward she poked her head into the dining area.

"Oooh!" she squealed.

Blake crossed over to her. "What? Where?"

"There," Alex replied as she pointed at Kenn and JJ. "There they are."

Before Blake could reply, she flipped her sunglasses back down over her eyes, tugged at his arm, and dragged him to the other end of the foyer.

They stepped around a family of four—a mom, dad, a girl who looked to be about twelve, and a very desolate-looking young man who obviously was a teenager—in the process.

"Come on, we've got to snag that booth before the maître d' gives it away." She picked up the pace, grabbed two menus from the side of the podium as she passed it—and dragging Blake every step of the way—furtively walked, using exaggerated tip-toed steps to the first artificial tree she found.

"Thank God this section of the place is lined with

these trees," she whispered to Blake, looking ahead to where the empty booth was.

"Spaghetti sounds good—but then filet sounds bloody good, too." Apparently, he didn't hear a word she had spoken.

She took her menu which had been covering her face as she walked and bopped him on the head with it.

"Focus, Blake, focus. Place the menu on the side of your face, like this." She grabbed it out of his hands, closed it, and put it against his cheek to hide his identity.

"Now, we'll tip-toe over to the next tree. Quietly but quickly." Alex raised her left leg as if she were marching—only silently and slower, and much more deliberately than a march.

Blake sighed dramatically. "Is this really necessary?"

"Of course, it is. All the great spies have approached their targets this way." She named some of the greatest spy duos in history.

"They're all TV characters," he complained.

She pushed a branch aside as she passed it, then let it go. The branch snapped back into its previous position, smacking her fellow spy in the face.

"Ouch. Watch it. And, just for your information, the last two are cartoon characters, for crying out loud."

"And we're two fictional characters from a romance novel. What's your point?"

"No point, I guess. No point at all."

Finally, they slinked their way over to the booth across from JJ and Kenn. They hurriedly slid into the benches.

"Just in time." Alex said. And not a moment too soon. The maître d' had reached the booth with the family of four. He was startled to discover it already occupied.

"Who are..." he began. He stopped in midsentence, displaying all the grace and confidence of a true professional and steered his diners to the next booth, as if nothing out of the ordinary had occurred.

On his return to the podium, he glared at the couple. She sweetly smiled back; Blake tipped his hat.

"Here, hurry. Open your menu and hold it up to hide your face." She opened Blake's menu for him and stuck it in front of his face.

"Again?"

"Yes, again."

He dutifully obliged. He waited a moment, then stuck his head out of the side of the large book-like menu.

"Psst! Alex." Her pose identical to his, she strained to hear JJ's conversation with Kenn.

"Psst! Sweetheart," he repeated.

"What?" The exclamation came out a little louder than she had intended. Then she whispered, "Can't you see I'm trying to listen?"

"Quite frankly, I can't see a bloody thing with this menu in front of me like this."

She fleetingly poked her head out of her menu. "That's a good thing. That means they can't see you." Her head bobbed back behind her makeshift fortress.

"I'm still going to have the spaghetti." He laid the menu down. "Garçon! Garçon!" he suddenly called out, holding his right hand above his head, and snapping his fingers.

"Don't!" She frantically tried to shove the menu back in his face and reached for his arm to pull it down.

Chapter 37

"Have you any idea what you're going to order?" JJ asked, as she looked over the candlelit table. She still couldn't believe she was on a real date, giving romance a second chance.

"Everything sounds so good—" Kenn began.

"Garçon! Garçon!" The man in the booth across from them shouted again. Kenn laughed at the cartoonish character.

"What a comical pair," he said, then paused. "There's something oddly familiar about them. I think I know them."

JJ looked their way, and gasped.

"You look like you've just seen a ghost," Kenn said. "Are you okay?"

"Yeah, yes, I'm fine." She continued to stare at the booth directly across from them.

"Oh, for heaven's sake. Isn't that…" He jumped up with enthusiasm and bounded over to the couple.

JJ quickly picked up her menu to hide her face. "Has everyone completely lost their minds?" she said out loud. A part of her couldn't watch the impending encounter. Yet, another part of her was fascinated by the events. She peeked out the side of the menu, hypnotized in a mystified horror.

Just as Kenn approached the booth, the maître d' came into sight, walking with a purposeful

170

determination. But Hawkman didn't come alone this time. Hustling up from behind, trying hard to keep up with his long-legged strides were Mario and Luigi. For every step Hawkman took, the brothers took three.

"Them." Hawkman dramatically swung his arm, pointing his long, bony finger at Alex and Blake, looking over his half-glasses. "*They* should not be there."

She watched Alex fidget in her seat, adjusting the menu in a vain attempt to hide her face. Either the finger of fate carried some unnamed magic power that caused her to wriggle uncontrollably or she was trying to make herself as inconspicuous as possible. The former seemed unlikely, and the latter nearly impossible, JJ thought ruefully.

"I'm sorry," Mario said, "but you'll have to leave the restaurant." Mario tried to present his best stern look. Luigi stood right behind him, hands on his hips, as if confirming the severity of the situation.

"Yes," Luigi said, "you'll have to leave the restaurant."

"Why?" Kenn asked.

"Oh, Mr. Yaki, are these friends of yours?" It was evident Mario was searching for an escape hatch.

"Yes, Mr. Yaki," Luigi parroted. "Are these friends of yours?"

Her anxiety at the situation evaporated when she heard her date being referred to as "Mr. Yaki." Thinking it best if she jumped in, she hurried to the table.

"Excuse me," she said, addressing the owners. "This is my cousin, Alex, and her fiancé Blake."

Alex gave the owner a small, meek finger wave, as she continued to hide behind the menu. "Hello?" she offered.

Mario and Luigi smiled and finger-waved back. Hawkman's posture, however, clearly indicated he stood steadfast in his displeasure with the whole situation.

"Alex, you didn't tell me you and Blake were eating here tonight," JJ said.

She then turned to the owners. "She didn't tell me they were eating here tonight."

"She didn't tell her," Luigi repeated to Mario. "Nobody told her."

Mario momentarily looked helpless. Hawkman glared down at him demanding their removal. But everyone else gave him sad puppy dog eyes.

"What the hell," she muttered to herself, "the evening is already ruined."

Loud enough so everyone could hear, she voiced the offer, her voice cracking as she spoke. "Alex, Blake, why don't you sit with Kenn and me. Of course, that is if it's okay with you, Mario." She looked at the brothers.

Luigi brightened, applauding her offer. "Why don't you sit with them?" he said with relief. Then he paused and added, "Of course, if it's okay with you, Mario."

Quite frankly, at this point, she was more concerned about Hawkman's opinion than Mario's. She could still feel the maître d's predator stare. Now, she felt as if she were a mother rabbit protecting her bunnies.

The owner, however, appeared quite relieved to have found a compromise.

"Why, of course," Mario exclaimed, evidently relieved to have the situation defused. "That's wonderful."

Then, looking up at the maître d', he said, "Lesley, see to it that Ms. Yaki's table is complete for four. And make sure they get another bottle of the finest wine in our cellar." Turning to JJ, he added, "On the house, of course. And Mrs. Yaki, I had no idea they were related to you. Please accept our apology."

Her romantic spirit sagged. Clearly all hopes of a quiet dinner alone with Kenn had vanished.

Alex gave a child-like can-I-really-go look to JJ, who nodded slowly. The fictional couple tore out of the booth and beat JJ and Kenn to their own table. They talked animatedly about their dinner choices.

Kenn appeared to enjoy the situation. JJ, however, felt things slipping totally out of control. She knew the night would get worse before it took a turn for the better—if it would ever take a turn for the better.

The server efficiently set the table for two more, left briefly, then returned with another bottle of wine.

"Compliments of the owners," he said as he uncorked the bottle. Pouring a small portion in Kenn's glass, he waited while Kenn tasted it. He nodded indicating his acceptance and the server poured everyone a glass.

"Wait, no one take a sip yet." Blake jumped up nearly toppling his chair. "I propose a toast. To all that is good in the world. To lifelong friendship." And then looking down at Alex, he said a little quieter, "And to finding your true love."

Alex blushed. JJ nearly dropped her glass, and Kenn merely agreed. "Cheers," Kenn added. The glasses clinked together, and all took a sip.

Blake drank his down like a sailor on leave. "So, Professor Cooper, I have a couple of questions about what we discussed in class this week. I was wondering if you could expand on—"

Before he could finish his sentence loud noises from

across the restaurant interrupted him. It was, well, at first it was hard to tell what it was. Three men were setting up sound equipment. "Oh, good," Alex said. "A live band. How romantic." She quirked an eyebrow and looked at JJ.

"They don't appear to be your run-of-the-mill lounge act," JJ commented. "The two are dressed in the customs of the Orthodox Jews with peyos, but..."

Blake interrupted her. "Their what?"

"Peyos. The long, curled sideburns they wear. That's what they're called."

"Oh."

Kenn continued her thoughts. "But they're also wearing sombreros. Hardly Orthodox Jewish head coverings."

"And look, the third man," Alex said, "is dressed in the sombrero and serape."

Mario sprinted, seemingly from out of nowhere, to the microphone the men had set up.

"Ladies and gentlemen, *Mario and Luigi's Italian Bistro* is proud to present to you—straight from Brooklyn, New York—the most talented Jewish Mariachi Polka Band in all the land. This talented trio really needs no introduction. So, I'll let them do what they do best: play their own special brand of music."

JJ heard a stifle of a noise from Kenn. She looked over to find him trying hard not to laugh. Looking at him she couldn't help but giggle.

"Heck, the finest in all the land," she said, "the only band in all the land is more like it."

The musical trio had one accordion and two pairs of maracas. They introduced themselves to the diners. "I'm Shell," said the taller of the two orthodox-looking men.

"And I'm Ira," said the other.

"My name," said the third with a distinct Latino accent, "is José."

José picked up the accordion and began to play. Shell and Ira played the maracas.

While the band played various polka tunes, the foursome ordered their meals. Dutifully, the server read back their entrees. "The two ladies are having Chicken Marsala," he said. "And we have a spaghetti dinner for one gentleman and a spaghetti dinner and a filet for the other." He looked at Blake who nodded enthusiastically.

"Wow, I don't think I ever heard that song played on an accordion before," Blake said, as the polka music suddenly morphed into a Jewish folk tune.

"And with good reason," Kenn added between outbursts of laughter.

Then Shell and Ira began singing. Much to their surprise, the floor in front of the trio quickly filled with diners. Forming a circle, they began to dance the traditional steps.

JJ watched as Mario and Luigi, who stood on the side, applauded with apparent delight. Then she saw Mario poke his brother in the ribs with his elbow and point at her and her companions. They toddled over as quickly as their stubby legs allowed and pulled them to the dance floor. With Luigi on one end of the foursome, and Mario on the other, they cut into the circle.

She immediately realized that joining an already rapidly dancing circle took skill, a skill she evidently failed to develop. She stumbled several times, nearly finding herself on her knees before she could keep up. She realized she probably would never conquer the steps. She prayed she never needed to.

But then she noticed Blake. He appeared to effortlessly and easily master the exact steps needed. *How did he do that?* He was more agile than he was in his mascot finger costume, that's for sure.

While she observed Blake, she got hopelessly behind on the steps herself and scrambled to get back into rhythm before she got run over by the other dancers. I can see the headlines, now, she thought: *History Professor Trampled To Death In Dance.*

What a way to go.

"Ouch!" Someone had stepped on her foot.

Kenn shrugged. "Sorry, I'm new to all of this." The boyish look on his face prompted a smile and a sudden lifting of her mood. In that instant she caught a glimpse of the real Kenn. And she knew without a doubt she had fallen in love. It felt incredibly exhilarating to admit. But it also felt bone chillingly scary. She knew her life would never be the same.

Chapter 38

"I think I've got it," JJ said to Kenn, as they circled around for what seemed like the umpteenth time. She found herself unusually proud of mastering the steps. She also loved the feel of Kenn's hands over hers.

"Hey, look." Kenn raised their hands toward Mario and Luigi. "Hawkman over there wants to cut in."

"Who knew he liked music?" She concentrated on her steps. She discovered she couldn't dance and talk at the same time.

The maître d' sprinted outside the circle as it appeared he wanted to cut in between Mario and Luigi. They were oblivious to him. He tapped Mario on the back and the owner slowed long enough to pull him into the circle. His large smile grew even more.

Hawkman's entrance into the dance circle proved problematic. He kept tripping over his long legs. He bent at the waist, as if he were trying to talk to Mario. She saw him finally get low enough to speak. She couldn't hear what he said over the loud music and apparently Mario couldn't either because he kept shaking his head.

Just then the song ended, as he screamed and pointed, "The real Teri Yaki is here!"

His words reverberated throughout the restaurant. All eyes were on him. Including JJ's. Fear coursed through her body. Her eyes followed the direction of his hand and she saw a tall, heavy-set woman in a tight-fitting black dress, a black cape draped about her. She was standing near their table.

JJ froze. She watched in horror as Mario went up to her. She handed him a card and announced. "Yaki. Teri Yaki. Food columnist for the *Bell Wyck Tribune*. The *Bell Wyck Bowl*, you've undoubtedly have heard of me."

"But if you're Teri Yaki, then who's..." Mario turned and stared at JJ.

She and Kenn exchanged looks. Dread crept up JJ's spine.

"Bloody bad timing." Blake reached for Alex's hand.

"Maybe we should have told them," JJ said.

Kenn shook his head. "Too late to fix that now."

"Who are you then?" Mario pointed his stubby finger at her.

She couldn't speak. Alex mewled.

Blake, wide-eyed and red-faced, grabbed Alex's hand and yelled, "Run! Run for your lives!"

Kenn took JJ's arm and they dashed to the foyer, closely followed by Alex and Blake.

"That's fine with me," Blake said, his hair bouncing to the rhythm of his sprinting. When he reached the exit, he stopped and turned.

"I've had better wine."

Chapter 39

They didn't stop running for nearly two blocks. Finally, Kenn halted, took several deep breaths, and looked behind them. "I don't think anyone is following us. The maître d' is probably busy fawning all over the real Teri Yaki."

"I wonder how she liked the Jewish Mariachi Polka Band," JJ said.

Alex and Blake were bent over at the waist, trying to catch their breath.

"Wait," Blake said, a look of consternation on his face, "We didn't even get our dinner. We were cheated."

"Blake!" Everyone roared.

"Okay, so maybe we weren't cheated, but I'm hungry."

"Come to think of it, so am I," said Alex.

Kenn looked at JJ. "I did promise you a dinner. We never did quite get that far."

They ducked into a nearby small diner, *Happy Days*. It wasn't as elaborately furnished as the Italian restaurant, but odds were good they wouldn't get thrown out, either. The eatery, an old trolley car, was updated in a kitschy style to look like you stepped back into time to the 1950s. The décor, though, created more of a worn-out look of the decade than a shiny, bright celebration of it.

They slid into a booth and ordered.

****

"But you got to admit," Blake said, two hands clutching tightly to a giant burger, "the food is decent."

The others nodded. "Even the coffee isn't that bad." JJ picked up the white mug and took another sip.

Blake and Alex sat on one side of the booth, a red vinyl covering that had several tears in it. JJ and Kenn sat on the other. She reveled in the intimacy of sitting close to the sensual man. In some ways, the moment felt more intimate than any of the time spent at Mario and Luigi's.

His thigh lay close to hers, just barely touching it. The touch was feather light and she barely felt the connection, but it sent chills up her spine. She wondered if he was doing it purposefully. She wondered, too, what he was feeling at the moment. She knew one thing: she was thankful that conversation was at a premium. She was too distracted soaking in these long-lost feelings to participate in any form of small talk.

The diner was empty of customers except for the four of them. Watching her fictional pair, she knew exactly what plans they had for the rest of the evening. Alex took notice of even the smallest of Blake's gestures. Blake, uncharacteristically quiet, sat close to his love, as he playfully ran his hands through her hair.

Unusually content, she took another sip of her coffee and leaned back in the booth. Out of the corner of her eye, she glanced at Kenn. He too seemed lost in his own thoughts. She whispered in his ear, "A penny for your thoughts."

His face went from a contemplative look to a slight, almost sly, smile, starting with his lips and continuing on to the corner of his eyes, making him look more boyish than usual.

"Oh, I really don't think you want to know." He gently placed his hand on her thigh. She involuntarily gasped in response to the warmth, tenderness, and the sensuous pleasure of the touch.

"I can't tell you now," he said, winking. "But I promise to let you in on my thoughts the moment we leave."

"Hmm, sounds provocative."

He took a long, deliberate gulp of his coffee, picked up the check, glanced at it, and then casually tossed several bills on the table as the tip. He quickly headed toward the cash register to pay for all four meals. Alex and Blake rose slowly, still gazing into each other's eyes and now holding hands. She rose from the booth, too, her eyes more concerned with every move Kenn was making than what the heroine and hero of her novel were doing.

Kenn turned after paying, walked up to her, and wrapped one arm about her waist. She felt her body slowly sink into his, an unexpected second wave of sensuality rushed over her. She savored the intimate familiarity that comes to couples with ease after they've spent time together. *How could this have happened so quickly?*

While she hadn't thought they had spent that much time together, she quickly recalled the cadence, the pace, and the perfect timing they'd experienced the past several weeks teaching together. They went from adversaries to true partners, she thought—and dare she even think it—even more. And they did that in a relatively short amount of time. The prospect she could be entering a new level in this relationship on both the emotional and physical planes both excited and frightened her.

Once outside the diner, Alex and Blake walked arm in arm gently staring into each other's eyes, softly touching the other's cheek. Blake tenderly lifted Alex's long hair, stopped momentarily, and sensuously kissed her neck. Just watching the scene ignited something in JJ that had lain smoldering for years. Her characters were so in love, and she was so very delighted for them. She was ready to have that type of relationship with Kenn.

Wrapped in Kenn's arms was an experience she had not expected but welcomed. He slowed his pace.

"We'll let them get a little ahead of us," he whispered. "I don't think they even know we're behind them."

"You're thinking again, Professor Cooper."

"Yes, I am. But I'm hesitant to put my thoughts into words. I don't want you to get the wrong idea."

He pulled her closer, kissing the top of her head. Goosebumps ran down her arms, an electric shock shooting through her body. All from a simple kiss on top of the head.

He stopped, turned her so they were facing each other, and kissed her on the lips. Hesitantly at first, but when she didn't protest, it grew more passionate. She returned the ardor with a desire not to let the moment end.

They stood there exploring each other, discovering the delights of the other, neither of them wanting to stop, hungry for more. She finally admitted she had an appetite pent up inside her.

Chapter 40

Kenn and JJ stood outside the door of his home. She wasn't exactly sure how they'd got there. It didn't matter. Kenn held her close with one arm as his other hand unlocked the door. His tenderness coursed through her body.

Pushing the door open, he looked down at her and quietly affirmed, "This feels so right."

She looked at him, wrapped in a sense of peace and sensuality, and nodded. "Yes, yes it does."

He led her through the living room and hallway and into his bedroom. She paid scant attention to the darkened room. Instead, they embraced again, melting into each other with an ease and familiarity of two people who had known each other forever. At that moment, she couldn't even think of what her life was like before he'd entered it.

Kenn's lips gently caressed her neckline as she ran her hands through his hair. Cupping his strong hand behind her neck, he looked down at her with a tenderness that she realized had been missing from her life. In the instant she looked deep within his eyes, as if searching his soul, his lips gently brushed hers. Soon the easy touch pressed into a more sensuous kiss.

Parts of her body responded with exotic feelings she had forgotten were even possible. They were locked in this passionate stance for a few moments. Then he reached down to unbutton her blouse, purposely and ever so slowly brushing his hands across her breasts. Chills ran down her body. She involuntarily, unconsciously spread her legs a bit, already gripped in physical anticipation of what lie ahead. She gasped and closed her eyes. It had been ages since a man had touched her in this way.

She reached down, gently undressing him, starting with his buttons, and continuing with his pants. He, in turn, removed her skirt. His lips again explored her mouth. Before she realized it, they were in the bed, their bodies tangled together, each discovering the delight of stirring the other to near frenzy.

His hand quivered momentarily before he massaged her breasts. He lowered his head and burrowed deeply and securely into them. She moaned breathlessly, feeling an orgasmic seismic reaction down into her pelvis.

Her heart felt as if it would burst, as her pelvic area rose in response. Kenn's fingers moved slowly downward, gently caressing and teasing the area.

She lost herself in him, delighting in the slow sensuality. When Kenn shifted his position and tentatively entered her, she gently encouraged him. The action gave her a sacred joy, a moment of bliss transcending any emotion she'd ever felt. She reveled in the hallowed feeling of Kenn inside her and the spiritual sanctity of the moment.

****

The morning light woke Kenn. He turned to find JJ leaning on an arm gazing at him. "You look peaceful when you sleep," she said.

"Good morning, sweetheart. Allow me to make you some breakfast. I whip up a mean omelet if I say so myself."

"How can I resist such an offer?"

The harsh sound of his phone on the nightstand jerked them out of their serene state. Instinctively, he reached for it.

Even before he had a chance to say hello, he heard his mother's voice. "Mom, this is a bad time, I can't talk right now," his tone low. He glanced at JJ, who looked as if she were trying hard to suppress laughter.

"What do you mean, it's a 'bad time'?" He was sure that JJ could hear the conversation without straining. "It's Sunday morning, for God's sake, what could you possibly be doing on a Sunday morning?"

"I'm busy right now."

"Why are you whispering? What's wrong with you?"

He felt his brows knit as he glanced over at JJ. The bizarre nature of the situation must have been too much for her, because she jumped up—beautifully naked, he noted—and moved as far away from the conversation as possible. She stopped when she was up against the bedroom door, nearly doubled over trying desperately to suppress her laughter. Her effort was futile.

"Oh, my heavens, son, do have someone there with you?"

He stumbled over his words, trying to be non-committal. But his mother, evidently, surmised the situation quickly. "You do. You had a date last night that continued into the morning."

"Oh son, please tell me you and JJ finally got together."

"Mom, I really don't want to talk about it now. It's a very awkward conversation."

"You can't hide anything from your mom. I'm sure JJ's there. Oh, Kenn this is so wonderful. I'm just so happy."

"Mom, I really have to go." He glanced at JJ, who was laughing even more, if that were possible. *Not quite how I expected this morning to go.*

"Oh, son, please give my best to JJ, tell her I can't wait to meet her and—"

Click. Kenn pressed the "end" button, placing the phone back in its cradle.

He tried to look irritated, but one glance at JJ's enjoyment of his predicament prompted him to laugh as well.

"So much for privacy," he said, trying hard to contain his own amusement.

They sat at the dining room table, a full complement of breakfast foods on their plates. Kenn was in his robe and JJ in one of his long dress shirts, the hem hitting the bottom of her hips.

He watched as she ate and wondered what was on her mind. It didn't take long for her to reveal it.

"I guess last night proves I've been a fool. But it also changes our relationship now."

"I know. I hope you agree it changes it for the better."

She looked at the ceiling. Her hesitation worried him. "Yes, I do agree. But…" She closed her eyes. Kenn waited for the rest of the sentence. "It's such a big step. It's been a long time since I've trusted anyone like I trust you."

"Oh, I'm not about to disappoint you, sweetheart."

Chapter 41

"I don't understand it." Alex grabbed a handful of
popcorn from the bowl she and Blake shared. Curled up
on the couch, they had another evening to themselves. It
had become an increasingly common situation as JJ
spent more time with Kenn.

"Well, Scarlett is a complex character, and the civil
war era is fraught with complexities." Blake seemed
absorbed in the classic movie they were watching.

"That's not what I'm talking about. Don't you see
it?" She had grown increasingly frustrated over the last
several weeks.

"See what?" Blake picked up some popcorn. His
eyes never leaving the television screen.

"I'm talking about JJ and Kenn. I'm talking about
us." She stood and ran a hand through her hair. "It
appears the woman who was kind enough to give me the
love of my life has found her own love." She paused and
stared at Blake. It took her a moment to realize he didn't
see the significance in the fact.

"So why aren't we home? That was the theory,
right? She finds the love of her life and—poof—we're
home."

He nodded. Just when Alex was sure he wasn't
paying attention, he smiled, grabbed the remote, and
fiddled with it.

"Watch this, love." His voice spewed enthusiasm.

Even his hair bounced.

"The movie?"

"No, this." He pulled her down on the couch next to him, seemingly oblivious to popcorn flying everywhere. He aimed the remote at the television and returned to a previous point in the streaming

"A commercial. That's a commercial. You want me to watch a commercial?"

"Shh! Yes, I do. I think we've found our method of returning home." He flashed her a heart-melting smile.

"I'm going to replay it one more time. Watch closely. Listen even more closely to what the lady says at the end."

She watched patiently. She loved him fiercely, but sometimes he made little sense. She feared this would be one of those times. She couldn't fathom how a stupid television commercial could be their ticket back to their world.

The commercial showed a typical harried housewife rushing through her day. Children. Husband. Those bratty kids again…

"What snotty-nosed brats they are. Our kids aren't going to act like that."

He froze in place and fumbled the remote control. "Hadn't thought about kids yet, love." He quirked an eyebrow.

"Well, how many do you think you're going to want…?"

"Shh! This is the part."

She swore his voice quivered. But she didn't know if it was the excitement at the prospect of getting home or the nervousness of thinking about having children.

"Watch her now."

"Yeah, she's climbing into a tub to take a bubble bath. So?"

"Listen to what she's saying here." He adjusted the volume.

"Calgary, take me away."

"Yeah so…" She strung out the last word, hoping he would fill in the rest.

"So? So?" Blake stood, his eyes wide. "If it works for her and takes her to a different place, why can't it work for us? Why can't it take us home? We just go to the store, buy some Calgary bath crystals, and…"

She was no longer listening. She had sprung up from the couch and run to the bathroom. "Come on, baby," she said, as she rummaged through the cabinet under the sink. "Mama needs to get home." She threw items about.

She waved the box of bath crystals at him when he finally caught up with her.

She watched as he ran out of the room.

"I'll get the towels," he hollered from the hallway.

Then she heard him in the kitchen. It sounded like he was tearing it apart. *What on earth is he doing in there?* On his return, he had the towels tucked under his arm. There was a bottle of champagne in his left hand and two glasses in his other.

"We might as well toast the moment." She sensed a triumphant attitude as he stood there. A man who had a plan, confident in its success.

Flushed with the excitement of the moment, she drew the water while Blake poured the bath crystals into the tub.

"More. We need more. We've got a long way to go to get back home." She tilted her head. "Actually, I'm not sure how long of a way it is in physical miles…but it sure seems like light years."

She looked back at Blake, clearly unimpressed. "More. More. Don't you dare be a wimp about this."

She took hold of his arm, turning it upward so the remainder of the crystals in the box fell into the tub. "There. That should do it, don't you think?"

"You just dumped three-quarters of a box of bath crystals into the tub."

"Yeah, well, I want to be sure this works. The more-is-better theory."

"Oh." Blake tilted his head. "It does go against the grain of the less-is-more theory now, doesn't it?"

She paid him scant attention. She was already stripping her clothes off.

"Blake. Take those clothes off, baby. I want to get home sometime today." Impatience raised Alex's voice to a mouse's squeal.

She watched as he tore off his T-shirt, tossing it mindlessly. It landed in the bathroom sink. He fumbled with his belt, hastily unbuckling it. His fingers worked quickly to unsnap his jeans. Then he grabbed his zipper, tore the latch down, and wiggled out of them, his hips doing double time to help drop them down.

Next, he tore his underwear off. He was about to take a step into the tub when Alex said, "Focus, Blake, focus. Those socks gotta come off, too."

"Oops. Haste makes waste."

Nearly naked herself, she glanced just by chance at the tub. The faucet was still running and the water threatened to overflow at any moment. She quickly bent over to turn the water off. Bubbles covered everything, the water in the tub, and the floor underneath, and the area surrounding the old claw tub.

They stood there stark naked, looking at the tub, bubbles seemingly growing by the minute. Blake grabbed her hand and eased her into the tub, her weight displacing some of the water, causing it to spill out onto the floor. He then turned around to snatch the champagne and the two glasses.

"A glass for my fair lady." She held the vessel while he poured. Then he climbed in. Pouring himself a glass, he placed the champagne bottle on the floor amid the soap bubbles.

"To home," he toasted.

"To home. And love," Alex squealed in return. They both gulped down the alcohol. Then Alex announced, "On the count of three—our new mantra, one, two, three: Calgary, take me away!"

Alex closed her eyes. Her muscles tightened in anticipation of the indescribable transformation she was about to experience going from the chapters of JJ's love story back to the pages of her own.

A beat passed. She opened her eyes. Instead of the familiar setting of their own world, they were still in JJ's tub.

"That's okay." Alex's eyes filled with tears, her voice shaky—nearly cracking. But still she smiled. "Let's try it again."

Blake reached down, took the champagne bottle, and poured two more glasses of bubbly. Again, they toasted. "To home. To love." And after they drank the champagne, they shouted the phrase. A little louder this time.

She closed her eyes once more and again her muscles tightened at the expectation of going home. She waited a moment, then opened her eyes. Nothing had happened. She and Blake were still in the tub. Still surrounded by what seemed to be acres of bubbles.

Even though the attempt failed, she brightened a bit. "Maybe we're supposed to say it three times like in that one movie?"

"Right-O. Bloody good thinking." Under stress, Blake's English accent became more pronounced.

Blake poured even more champagne. "Oops. That's the last of the bottle," he said. They downed it quickly and began to chant—

An angry knock at the bathroom door interrupted them. "I wonder who that could be?" Blake asked. Alex giggled.

"Blake! Alex! What in blue blazes are you guys doing in there?" JJ said.

"Well," Blake offered, "that answers the question of who's at the door." He hiccupped.

"I guess she came home early from her date," Alex said, as she giggled.

JJ opened the door and stared at the pair.

"My floor! My bathroom floor is flooded with soapy water. What are you two trying to do now?"

She glanced at the box of Calgary bath crystals laying on its side. Then, her eyes lingered at the equally empty champagne bottle.

"Never mind. I can only imagine. I want both of you out of there right now, the floor dried and you guys dressed, for crying out loud!"

JJ slammed the door on her way out.

Alex burst into tears.

Blake put a hand to his head. "I never knew such a small room could spin so fast."

Chapter 42

"Spending another weekend at Kenn's?" Alex asked, when she saw JJ set her overnight bag on the kitchen café table next to her messenger bag. JJ was pouring her to-go cup of coffee for the commute to the university. As much as she loved working from home as a romance writer, the commute to work felt good. She found joy in teaching.

But more than that, she found joy with a man she thought she despised. Her initial horror of working side by side with him had soon dissolved. She found they made a good, if not perfect, teaching pair. Their styles complemented one another, and as improbable as it seemed when she first met him, Kenn actually respected her views.

She secured the lid on her cup and pivoted. "As a matter of fact, I am." JJ couldn't help but smile at the thought of another weekend alone with Kenn. Even a few weeks ago, that question from Alex would have elicited a harsh response from her.

"And I owe it all to you. And Blake. Without your encouragement and persistence, I would never have gotten to know Kenn. I would have totally blown him off."

Alex beamed. JJ thought that must have been the ultimate compliment for a romance-novel character. She sighed. Alex had performed her assigned mission well.

She couldn't have foreseen any of this when she discovered them in her office. All the irritation the two had caused her in the last several weeks melted away. She had nothing but love for them.

Did she see a tear run down Alex's cheek? Then it dawned on her. Alex and Blake were still stuck in her world.

"I know you're ready to go home. I'm sure it will happen soon. I wish I could be more help to you with that."

She strode over and hugged Alex. She, too, teared up and began to cry.

At that moment, Blake walked in, his backpack slung over his shoulder, his hair still wet from a shower. "Are you..." He stopped in mid-sentence when he saw the two women embracing and crying.

She released Alex when she heard his voice. When she saw the stunned look on his face, she laughed. "I've never known you to be speechless before."

Alex went to him and wrapped an arm around him. She explained her frustration. "That was the theory, right? That when JJ found the love of her life, we would be able to return home."

Blake furrowed his brow. "What if..." he began to speak. "No, never mind."

"What if what?" Alex pressed him.

"No, that's not possible," he said, clearly lost in his own thought processes.

"Just tell us." She felt that any insight Blake had would be helpful. She couldn't imagine why he was so cryptic.

"Well, what if Kenn isn't JJ's true love?"

She blinked her eyes, as if that would help her

understand what Blake had just said. "That's impossible. Of course, he's my true love."

It was first time she had ever admitted it to herself. And it felt liberating.

****

Kenn poured his first cup of coffee Friday morning and sat at the kitchen table, where he had placed the book he was reading the night before. He opened it and continued reading as he sipped his coffee.

"I didn't see that coming," he said out loud, as he quickly turned the page. Kenn was nearly halfway through JJ's novel, *Love's Revenge*. He didn't dare tell her he was reading it—not after the way he went on about how all romance novels were trash. And he certainly couldn't tell her he really loved it. At least, not yet.

He did owe her a better apology than the one he awkwardly and hastily proffered in her office the first day of class. As he had come to know the woman and scholar she was, he realized he had a lot of baggage he needed to deal with. Starting with his unequivocal stance on literature.

"No wonder she wanted nothing to do with me," he mused. It was my own fault, he thought. *If she only knew that as soon as we were forced to teach in the same small area, I bought her books and started reading them. She is one talented writer.* He admitted there was more to romance literature than met the eye.

He glanced at the clock and realized it was time to put the book down—*but I still have to see what happens to Elenore*—and get dressed and go to campus. He reluctantly closed the book and stood. He carried it into his bedroom where he tucked it safely into the top drawer of his nightstand. He definitely didn't want JJ to find it the next time she visited.

And that would be—today. It's Friday. He smiled at the thought of another weekend with the wonderful woman. He stepped into the shower, his thoughts consumed with how much his life had changed in the past several months. From mourning the loss of his girlfriend Rain to celebrating his romance with JJ.

As he dried himself, he reluctantly admitted his mother had been right. Painfully right. He couldn't even begin to compare the two women. Rain had been fun. And Rain was a smart woman. But JJ was all of that. And more. She had a depth he had never seen in a woman before.

As one who had stubbornly dismissed the idea of fate, destiny, kismet—too many factors complicated that simplistic approach to life—meeting JJ had him rethinking the concept.

As he dressed, he smiled at the thought of his day. JJ in the morning, in the afternoon, and most wonderfully, in the evening. He had come to love his weekends.

He entered the kitchen, picked up his laptop case, and headed out the door.

Chapter 43

"Do you know what day it is?" Alex asked JJ as the three of them went through their ritual scrambling around the house getting ready to leave for campus one morning.

"Nope," JJ replied not missing a beat in her routine. "But I'll take a guess. Is it National-Take-Your-Portuguese-Water-Dog-To-Lunch Day?"

"No, it's your anniversary."

JJ abruptly stopped pouring her coffee and stared at Alex, who was checking the contents of her backpack.

"My anniversary?"

"Yup."

"And I was supposed to remember this anniversary commemorating I don't know what?"

"Yup. I thought you would, at least. After all, you're the romance author, not me."

"That's true," she said slowly, thinking carefully before forming her words. "But you are my romantic creation. Sometimes you view life a little differently than I do."

That seemed a much nicer way of saying she was a total romantic lunatic. But, heck, what can you expect? She normally lived inside the pages of romance novel.

"Ookaay…my one-month anniversary of what?"

Alex rolled her eyes to express the classic I-can't-believe-you're-asking-that.

"I can answer that in two words," Blake announced as he entered the room, clearly taking in more of his surroundings than he let anyone know.

"Grilled cheese." He paused as if he expected her to understand his answer.

When she didn't react, he said, "I see I'm going to have to use more than two words," he said, shaking his head. He sighed. "It's been exactly one month since you and Professor Cooper made passionate love for the first time."

"Blake!" JJ and Alex said.

"Well, it is." He shrugged his backpack over his right shoulder.

"And even you remembered this anniversary when I didn't?"

"No, not until Alex reminded me when we went to bed last night."

"You two were discussing my love life in bed last night? Is nothing sacred?"

"Sure. Many things are," Blake said. "But apparently not your love life."

She placed the lid on her to-go cup. "And what do you suggest I do with this information? Run and tell Kenn about it?"

"Well…" Alex's voice trailed off.

"No, I will not."

****

"Good morning, son." The familiar voice sang into Kenn's phone. Kenn was still dealing with the act of waking up. He had programmed his coffee pot to start brewing at six-thirty in the morning. The smell caressed its way to his bedroom. He still struggled, urging his body out of bed to pour a cup.

"Mom? Do you know what time it is?" He laboriously raised his body to a sitting position.

"Of course, I do, dear. Six-thirty. And I'm also aware of what day it is."

"Is it some type of holiday?" Kenn thought it was too early to play guessing games. But if it were some holiday he forgot and there were no school, then he could lounge in bed a bit longer. Betting it wasn't a national-close-the-school holiday, he tossed the covers off and began the trek to the kitchen. He knew he would need caffeine to help him deal with this conversation.

"It's your anniversary." Kenn pulled a cup out of the cabinet over the coffee pot. He inhaled its robust aroma.

"My anniversary?" He poured his coffee. Oh, yeah, he was going to need this.

"Technically, yours and JJ's."

"And what anniversary is that?" Kenn took a satisfying drink.

"It's been one month since you and she made love."

Kenn choked on his coffee, coughing loud and long.

"Kenn, are you all right?" He finished coughing, catching his breath long enough to speak.

"Mom, don't you think that's rather private information."

"It's not like I shared it with my book club or anything."

"No, but it's a bit unsettling my mother knows anything about my love life, let alone keeps track of it."

Before his mom could answer, he continued. "No, let me take that back. It's eerie." He clicked the phone off.

****

A month, JJ thought as she turned the engine over in

her car. She waited until Alex had backed the compact car out of the garage, then put the gearshift into reverse. After the initial delight of finally succumbing to making love, the month, she mused, had settled into a wonderfully, satisfying loving routine. One she thought she would never experience after the death of her husband.

She rarely spent an entire weekend at home. Either Friday or Saturday night (occasionally both) she spent at Kenn's. Usually, they shared a quiet dinner they had made together. Some stimulating conversation afterwards, then deep, sensual lovemaking before falling asleep in Kenn's arms.

The weekdays seemed to be just as fulfilling. The team-taught conspiracy course was a success beyond anyone's expectations. Not only were the students fully engaged in constructive, lively discussion, but Kenn respected her openness. While he didn't always agree with her conclusions, she knew he had come to admire her meticulous research. He respected her intellectually. Quite a turnaround from their first encounter.

And, JJ mused as she entered the faculty parking lot, there were those delightful lunches and cappuccino breaks at the Physics Café. They talked about anything— from news to office gossip, to quantum physics to spiritual matters.

The finishing touch of her life, though, was the ability to make time to work on her novel. She had developed a theory of her own regarding the return of Alex and Blake to the pages of their own book. She could only pray her theory worked. As much as she loved them, she knew they didn't belong in her world. And she knew Alex wouldn't find her true happiness until she was back in the pages of her own story.

****

As Kenn drove to campus, he had to admit the month had flown by in an amazingly satisfying way, even though it was disturbing that his mother was the one who pointed it out to him.

He had once thought he would never recover from the blow of his breaking up with Rain. He knew, though, when he saw JJ in the bookstore that day, she could be the one to change all that. He couldn't readily pin down his exact need to find his true love. He was only beginning to understand the implications of the term from reading his girlfriend's novels. He recalled the first impression he made on her: that of a pompous ass. Heck, how could it have been anything else?

He was relieved when through some amazing coincidences he was able to correct the situation. *Okay, so it wasn't the second impression at Rob and Nan's that changed her mind. Nor was it the third.*

Oh, please, he finally thought. *I'm one lucky pompous ass that she even gave me a chance.*

It's now been a month of utter perfection. Who saw that coming?

****

Blake thought Alex was unusually quiet on the way to the campus that morning. No talk of the cheerleaders or of her psych class. He wondered what she was thinking about. After all, her determination had paid off. JJ and Kenn were a couple.

"Okay." Alex finally broke the stillness of the ride. He was about to learn what was on her mind. "I'm beginning to worry about my latest theory on returning home."

"Why's that?" He looked at her. "And, by the way, what is your latest theory?"

"You know darn well what it is. I figured that once JJ and Kenn found each other our work here would be completed and we'd be magically transported back to the pages of our book."

He took a deep breath, savoring the delicious cadence and natural lyrical tone of her voice.

"They've been together for a month now. Plenty of time to know they were made for each other. So why aren't we home yet?"

He thought he detected a tear or two in her eyes. He couldn't tell her that he felt frustrated, too. His ideas to get them home always fizzled. He had tried hard to get her back to where her heart lay. But it never worked out. Failure was a new experience for him. He seldom failed in the novel. *I don't like it one bloody bit.*

In that moment, he felt compelled to offer her some intellectual, logical explanation of her theory. But sadly, he was at a loss. He actually thought hers was as good a thesis as any. All he could do was offer her reassurance.

"We'll get home, love. I promise you that." Now he just had to come up with a plan. Again.

Chapter 44

Kenn swung his car into the faculty parking lot by the history department building, got out, and listened for the beep as he locked it.

He was still smarting from his mom's knowledge of his one-month anniversary with JJ. And highly embarrassed that she had used the first night they made love as an anniversary marker. Parents definitely shouldn't know that type of information about their children.

At least, it's staying within the family, he thought, it could be so much worse. He walked into the departmental office before going to his own. He retrieved documents from his mail cubicle, then turned to talk to Deb.

"Beautiful flowers. Who sent them to you?"

Deb looked up from the computer screen with the smile of a Cheshire cat.

"Your mom," she said, raising her eyebrows.

"Why did my mother send you flowers?"

"So I could give them to you."

"Give them to me…?"

He knew there was a story behind this. And he was afraid to find out. He sighed and finally said, "Okay, I give up. Why is my mother giving me flowers?" *Beautiful red roses at that.*

"If you want to truly get technical," Deb said, as her

eyes danced with glee, "they're really not for you."

Kenn was irritated with her coyness. He knew the secretary well and had been through similar conversations. Of course, none involving flowers from his mother. The longer she strung out the conversation, the bigger the zinger at the end. He shook his head as he rubbed the back of his neck.

Sighing, he asked, "Do I even want to know who they're for?" But he thought he already knew the answer.

"JJ."

Kenn knew full well he shouldn't ask the next question, but something inside of him urged him on.

"Did she happen to tell you why I would want to give JJ flowers?"

"Oh, yeah. She sure did, Professor Cooper."

Now her eyes gleamed with devilish delight. "She told me this was your one-month anniversary of you and Professor St. Clair making—"

"Don't go there." He interrupted before she could get the words out. "I'm sure she was graphic in her explanation."

Deb nodded and grinned.

The secretary stood, picked up the vase, and handed it to him. He reluctantly accepted it, shoulders slumped, and headed for the door. He was already trying to find a way to explain all this to his girlfriend.

And wondered if she would still be his girlfriend at the end of this mess.

He knew she would explode. Hell, he wanted to. Their relationship started off badly, to say the least. And he knew she was hesitant to even give love another chance. As he walked out of the history department office, he knew that he might as well be wearing a bull's eye target.

****

JJ was stunned when Kenn walked in with a dozen red roses and wished her a happy anniversary.

"Have you been talking to Alex already this morning?"

"No, I haven't. Why?"

"No offense, but I really didn't expect you to even consider a month as an anniversary—let alone remember it with roses."

She hesitated, then decided the truth was the best route. "Actually, I wouldn't have thought of it if Alex didn't announce it this morning."

Kenn flashed his boyish smile at her. She knew immediately there was a story behind this present. He shifted his weight from one foot to the next, suddenly assuming the appearance of a shy schoolboy asking the most popular girl to the dance.

"If you're thinking I'll get angry because you didn't remember this date on your own, don't worry about that. I'm the romance author, and I didn't have it marked on my calendar. And you know how we romance novelists are."

She grinned as she cleverly reminded him of his opinion of "her ilk" on their first encounter.

He placed the vase on her desk. She watched as he nervously shoved his thumbs in his pockets, rocking back and forth on his heels. He clearly was not comfortable enough, she noted, to sit down.

She could just about read his mind, too. She knew he was weighing his options. If he admitted he didn't remember and admitted Alex reminded him, he feared her wrath. She was sure of that.

Her office acquired an eerie silence. "It wasn't Alex who reminded me. But someone did bring it to my attention." He spoke quietly. JJ thought he purposely spoke in a low voice, almost a murmur to muffle his answer.

"Well, then who reminded you reminded you?" she asked when several moments had passed.

He was blushing. That could only mean one thing.

"Your mother? Your mother reminded you of this anniversary?"

"Well…" He continued to rock on his heels.

She chuckled. "I remember her calling that Sunday morning. I can see her now, marking it down on her calendar."

Once he heard her answer, he took his thumbs out of his pockets and sat down. Finally, JJ thought.

"You're not furious my mother knows?"

"I know I should be, but the idea is so absurd that I think it's funny."

She paused, then, trying to credit him with something before he completely lost face, she said. "I do love the flowers you chose. They're beautiful."

"Yeah, well about those, uhm, well, they weren't completely my doing."

She raised her eyebrows. *The plot thickens.*

"Let me guess. Your mom had them delivered to you to give to me." She could easily see that happening and she didn't even know Mrs. Cooper that well. But it would be predictable Mom Cooper behavior.

"Not exactly. You know, hon. I'm having a hard time telling you this because I'm slightly afraid of your reaction. The story gets pretty involved. When you hear how I got these flowers, you're not only going to be embarrassed, but livid. And I'm afraid our one-month anniversary will also mark the end of our relationship."

Oddly enough, she realized she wasn't angry.

"The old me probably would be angry, but as much as I don't like it, I'm adjusting to the fact that our private lives have become a fascinating hobby for others around here."

"We seem to be everybody's favorite form of entertainment." He stood and paced behind the chair he had been sitting in,

"Is the chain of events that bad?"

He nodded. "You're going to find it embarrassing. You may even not want to talk to me ever again. And, quite frankly, I wouldn't blame you."

"What the hell. Bring it on." She took a deep breath.

"My dear mother called Deb Dilley yesterday, informed her of the occasion, and sent flowers directly to Deb for me to give to you."

He paused. Then, he quickly finished with the obvious. "She handed them to me this morning to give to you." He stood resolutely behind the chair, hands clenched on its back.

"Somehow, I'm not surprised by any of this." In fact, she discovered the chain of events actually amused her. She pushed her chair away from the desk and swiveled it around in a circle once, then stopped to talk.

"It could be worse, you know," she said to her love. "Dr. Chare could have been included in this loop."

A voice boomed from the door. "I have far too much information about your love life. I'm the department chair, so why do I feel as if I'm some kind of matchmaker? I'm out of here."

She scrunched her face, gave Kenn a bewildered

look, then crossing her arms on the desk, she buried her head in them. Her life was careening out of control.

She found it incredibly, insanely amusing.

Chapter 45

"There's an underlying universal truth behind this morning's curious twist of events," JJ said as she and Kenn walked to class, his arm lightly brushing hers. *A comfortable feeling but still incredibly arousing, even after a month of intimacy. There's something to be said for this life.*

"Can you guess what it is?"

"Hmm. That's a tough one. Going to give me a hint?"

"Nope. Just going to tell you. It proves that unexpected conspiracies are all around us. More than we think. We just fail to connect the dots."

"You think our month anniversary is a conspiracy? Does that mean our relationship is a conspiracy, too?"

Of course, it is, she thought. *My characters purposely jumped out of the pages of my novel to orchestrate this. But there's no way I can tell you that and still sound sane.*

She stopped, turning the ninety-degree angle necessary to face him. "Not the relationship, but our awareness of the anniversary. Really, would we even be talking about it if your mom and Deb weren't in cahoots with each other?"

"Cahoots? What a word."

"Yeah. It's a colloquialism meaning—"

"I know what it means." Kenn tilted his head

smiling broadly at her. *I wonder what he's thinking.*

She smiled back every bit as broadly, gazing up at his brown eyes. She could easily get lost in those gorgeous, deep brown eyes. She tried to put that out of her mind.

"You can't deny they were in cahoots, can you?"

"You got me there." He started walking again but she stood still as if frozen in place.

"Oh, my goodness. Speaking of cahoots, you don't think that Alex and Blake are cahooting, too?" She scurried to catch up to him, about twenty paces beyond her and tugged at his elbow.

"I just had a horrible vision of Alex and Blake presenting us with an anniversary cake or something in front of the entire class."

"Good grief, JJ. Get over the cahoots, will you. I can't imagine them doing something like that."

"We are talking about the same couple that wallpapered our classroom with *The Daily Digit's* front page?" She couldn't even bring herself to describe the event which was known campus-wide as simply, *The Kiss*.

He laughed. "They do love to embarrass you. Is that their goal in life?"

"It may seem like that—and there's even times I wonder that myself. But they really have nothing but good intentions. They've been worried about me burrowing into my novels for hours or days on end and not living my own life." *Their ultimate goal is to get you and me firmly established in a relationship. And it appears their cahooting is working. Go figure.*

They continued walking, then as if without warning the classroom door loomed in front of her. A tsunami of horror washed over her. Walking slower, as if treading through unknown territory, she approached cautiously.

"Here, you go first," she said, lightly pushing Kenn forward. "I've got your back."

She followed him closely as he stepped into the room, trying hard to be his shadow. She braced herself for cat calls, applause, or any other form of so-called congratulatory recognition. But it was unusually quiet in the room. Even the normal animated chatter between Alex and Blake was absent.

"Well, so far so good," Kenn whispered in her ear.

"I'm not comfortable with it. It's eerily quiet in here. Something's going to happen. I can feel it."

But as they engaged the class in the possible conspiracy angle in the Lincoln assassination, they let their guard down. Apparently, the news had not spread to their students.

The end-of-class bell rang, and she blew out a breath.

"We did it." Kenn, too, seemed visibly more relaxed.

"So it seems. Considering that other aspects of our relationship have been celebrated here, I'm counting today as a miracle."

She paused and tilted her head. "Should I light a candle and say prayers for nine days?"

"That's probably not necessary. But I am giving thanks to some unseen universal force that must be watching over us."

As the class trickled out, several students approached them. She flinched, absolutely certain they intended to extend anniversary congratulations. Momentarily, she panicked, wondering if she could make a dash out the door without being too conspicuous. *No, probably not.* She was quite relieved when they were asked questions about John Wilkes Booth.

Both she and Kenn were so engaged in the conversation, in fact, she hadn't noticed Alex and Blake hanging back waiting to talk to them as well. As soon the other students left, Alex approached her.

"Blake and I want to treat the two of you to lunch at the Physics Café today," she said. "I think today would be a perfect day to thank you two—and especially you JJ—for everything you've done for us."

JJ's radar went on high alert. Kenn's, though, seemed to have been turn off and ripped out.

"How nice. Why of course we'd love to come, wouldn't we, JJ?"

She nodded slowly, her eyes casting leftward to Kenn then returning to Alex's smiling face. She pasted on a smile of her own. She barely spoke above a whisper.

"Yes, how can we possibly say no?"

Then she raised her eyebrows and grimaced at Alex, who beamed back at her.

"Great." She bounced on her toes vigorously.

"Thanks, guys. Blake and I are looking forward to it. Aren't we, Blake?"

The usual loquacious Brit nodded without saying a word. But JJ thought his face warned of trouble ahead.

"Meet you at the café at noon."

Chapter 46

Kenn opened the door to the café for JJ, who took a few steps inside. Her feet refused to move any farther. With her eyes riveted to the front of the coffee shop, she felt the anxiety she tried to suppress all morning rise in her. She knew she was trapped.

"I do believe cahooting has soared to a whole new level," she said.

To her left, she saw the Jewish Mariachi Polka Band diligently setting up their equipment. Ira saw her and waved. "*Hola*," he said, his curly Jewish orthodox sideburns bouncing about.

José looked up and called, "*Shalom*!"

"Now, don't jump to conclusions, they could be here for an entirely different reason. Maybe Alvin and the guys thought they would bring music in to attract more customers."

"And this looks like the group to draw the college crowd?"

"JJ, Professor Cooper, over here." Alex bounded out of her chair and rushed toward them, her softly curled hair dancing. Her eyes sparkled with delight. Joy seemed to radiate from her. She decided Alex was firmly ensconced in her element. JJ shot a quick glance over at Kenn, who wore the I-think-we're-trapped look.

Alex took JJ's hand and led her to their table. Kenn quickly followed as they approached two tables pushed together to accommodate them all. Tables right in front of the band.

That's when JJ noticed them. She felt every muscle in her body tense, even muscles she didn't know she had. Deb and—*oh, my Lord, no!*—Dr. Chare were also seated at the table, enthusiastically talking with Blake. She heard the chair chortle. *He's the only man I know who actually can chortle.*

Kenn pulled out a chair for JJ, and as he helped her settle in, bent over close to her. "I now believe in the cahooting club." He sat down next to her.

"Hi, Dr. Chare," JJ said. "Fancy meeting you here. Deb." She nodded at the secretary. "Didn't really expect to see either of you here."

"My, my," the chair chuckled as he talked. "I wouldn't miss this for anything." *Did he have a mischievous gleam in his eye?*

"I'm going to tell Alvin we're all here." Blake quickly pushed his chair back and sprinted to the kitchen.

The trio of owners appeared with Blake tagging behind them. They carried two appetizers, the Onion String Theory and the Avogadro's 'mole dip and chips.

They placed the appetizers on the table and the band began to play. Every person at the table and eventually the entire café, which seemed remarkably crowded, sang happy anniversary to some tune she didn't recognize.

"Is there any way that I could use the shop's de-particlizer and just disappear for a while?" she asked Kenn.

As she sat, tears of frustration welled up. The accordion played flawlessly, as well as an accordion could, and the maracas kept shaking to the beat of the music. Her cheeks grew hot. She wondered what shade of red they would be before this nightmare was over.

She stole a quick glance at Kenn. He reached under the table for her hand and squeezed it tightly. Leaning in close to her, he whispered, "We'll get through this. We will."

"You trying to convince me or you?"

"Both of us, I think. I'm surprised my mother didn't have a hand in this." He spoke loudly enough so she could hear him over the music.

"No, this has my charac…I mean, my cousin's fingerprints all over it."

"Enjoy," Alvin encouraged them. "The entrée will be ready soon, specially created for Professors St. Clair and Cooper's anniversary."

Chare and Deb hungrily pulled the dip closer to them—just out of the reach of JJ and Kenn—while Alex and Blake snatched up and hugged the onion strings, leaving them helplessly watching as the two appetizers were eaten in what could only be considered record time.

"Hope you weren't hungry." JJ shrugged. "Appetizers don't seem to be in our immediate future."

"Mmm. Mmm. The guys make the best onion strings," Blake said between bites. "Don't you think, love?"

Love was in the middle of chewing a large mouthful of strings. She wiped her mouth with a napkin and nodded in agreement.

"Couldn't taste any better than this Avogadro's 'mole dip," the chair said. "The boys really outdid themselves with this appetizer."

"I didn't know the chair could eat with such gusto," Kenn said. "I think there's another side to him he never lets us see."

"Ta Da!" Alvin, Ted, and Simon finally brought the entrée.

"It looks like we each get our own plates." Kenn exhaled. "I'm relieved. I thought I might have to sit through this entire meal watching other people eat."

The owners set a plate in front of each guest. "Introducing our newest addition to the Physics Café menu. Spaghetti and meatballs. In honor of the professors one-month anniversary, we're calling it Quantum Entanglement."

The entire table—no, make that the entire place— cheered. JJ was only now recognizing the amount of planning and organizing her two characters had put into this moment.

She pressed her forehead against Kenn's arm. Quietly, she asked, "Is there any way we can leave now without anyone noticing?"

"No such luck, sweetheart."

"I'm not sure I even have an appetite," she said, as she looked around the café. It was at that moment she realized that not only were the members of her class there, but just about the entire men's pep squad and the cheerleaders.

"If that's the case, could I have your leftovers?" Blake asked.

"Ouch! Why did you kick me? What did I do now?" The words came out as a whine.

"It's JJ's anniversary, sweetheart. Not ours. She's the one who should be enjoying this. And she doesn't look like she is."

She had plastered herself against Kenn, her head securely nestled in the crook of his arm, her eyes glazed over.

"What's the problem?" Alex asked. "We thought you would like this celebration."

She raised her head, looked straight into Alex's eyes. "Did you really? How would you like it if your most personal moments were broadcast throughout the campus?"

"My life will soon be an open book," Alex said without hesitation.

"Literally," Blake added with a smile.

She watched as Dr. Chare grabbed another dinner roll from the middle of the table. "You really need to stop worrying about any of that, Professor St. Clair, and dig into that spaghetti. It's delicious, simply delicious."

"It really is," Deb added. "This puts *Mario and Luigi's* to shame." She took a sip of water before she added, "You're lucky to have such a great meal named in your honor."

She looked up at Kenn. He shook his head as his free hand covered his mouth. She pondered the situation she found herself in. How could everyone be okay with it?

She raised her head out of the safety of Kenn's arm and studied her pair of fictional characters.

"It doesn't bother you that your life is an open book, Alex?"

"No," she said, "it comes with the territory. You take life as it happens."

The full impact of what her characters said hit her.

My life will be an open book.

Literally.

They had spoken the truth. In fact, the entire purpose of her creating them was for the entertainment of others. She hoped that literally millions of people would know about Alex and Blake's love story.

217

What a fool I've been. Part of living is allowing others to see who you really are. Interacting with people.

Then she shot up out of her seat. "I finally get it," she announced as she pulled Kenn up out of his chair.

"You love me no matter what, even if right now I may embarrass the hell out of you?" She whispered in his ear.

"Nothing you could do can embarrass me, darling."

"Don't be too sure about that. But I want to give these people what they really came to see—a love story."

She pulled Kenn toward her, stood on her tip-toes, and whispered, "Get down here and give me one long, passionate kiss. I'm celebrating the fact my life is an open book."

As they embraced and kissed, she heard Dr. Chare gasp. *Or was he choking?* After a moment, the choking ended and she heard him repeat over and over, "I see nothing. I see nothing."

She heard a small amount of applause at first, then it steadily grew. By the sound of it the entire café was captivated by the moment.

But she refused to stop and look. Then she heard the scuffle of a chair and Alex saying, "Kiss me, you wonderful fool." She could only imagine where that led to. The applause and cheers were now deafening.

Then she realized the Jewish Mariachi Polka Band was playing the theme from that tragically romantic movie from 1970. It had taken her a moment to recognize it played on an accordion.

Finally, she pulled herself away from Kenn. She didn't think the reaction couldn't get any louder, but somehow it did. She took a quick bow and noticed Alex and Blake staring at her.

"Oh, we're not done, yet." She winked at them and then trotted over to the band. When she approached the music abruptly halted.

"How about that Jewish folk dance tune that you guys do so well? I feel like dancing."

****

JJ's body melted into Kenn's as she rested a leg over him and nuzzled her face into his chest. Even though they had already made love several times, she felt a desire to re-ignite their passion again. Kenn's strong arms brought her even closer. If ever two bodies could be one, if ever two people could be one, this was the moment, she thought.

He playfully fingered her breasts. The morning light streaking through the bedroom window told her they needed to prepare for class. Still, she hesitated to let go of him. They had left the unexpected anniversary lunch without anyone noticing. Ironic, she thought, but she wasn't in the least bit surprised.

"It's time, you know," she said, her eyes shut, still feeling the sweetness and tenderness and surge of sexual energy of the prior evening. The explosion which eventually settled into a satisfying gentle completion lingered with her and probably would throughout the day. This man certainly had it all.

"I know," he answered. But instead of distancing his body from hers, he enfolded her even closer. Then he tenderly traced his fingers over her lips. He smiled and whispered, "I think I'm having an epiphany," and confidently and passionately kissed her.

Every nerve in her body swelled. Her senses tingled with uncontrolled desire as she wrapped her leg ever tighter around his waist.

Sighing, he eased out of the kiss, holding her at arm's length. "It goes without saying, Dr. St. Clair, that you are the most beautiful woman I've ever seen but…"

"But?" She caught a glimpse of the twinkle in his eye that she loved so.

"You are also the most confusing. Those times when I really didn't mean to set you off, you ranted, raved, and raged at me. Then when I'm sure I'm about to feel your wrath, I discover an epiphany."

"Like yesterday?"

"Exactly," he said, as his hand gently caressed her shoulder. "I'm not complaining, mind you, but I felt sure that anniversary lunch signaled our demise as a couple."

"It almost did." She thought about the soul-crushing dread she felt when everyone sang that lame happy anniversary song. "But then Alex said something that put it all in perspective for me. And I realized what a pompous ass I've been about so many things."

"Mind sharing these words of wisdom? I'd love to hear them."

She bit her lower lip. *How to explain this without saying the cousins from Kansas were actually characters from her novel—and that within several months everyone would be reading about them.*

"I guess I just realized that if I'm going to have a life outside my novels, I've got to understand and accept that some areas are an open book. Instead of hiding and suppressing the details of my life and relationships, I need to follow Alex's example—and start enjoying every minute of them. Even the seemingly embarrassing ones."

A silence settled over the room. He turned his head to the side and stroked her hair.

"But I was terrified that epiphany would push you away. I felt when I kissed you at the cafe, I was risking our relationship."

"Nothing, but nothing could make me leave you, JJ. It took me too long to find you." He gave her another impassioned kiss.

"Class soon," she said, as her toes involuntarily curled, and her pelvic area eased closer to him.

"I know." Slowly he removed his lips from hers.

"I do have to run home and change clothes before I go to class. I may be calling it a bit close."

"We'll just have to solve that problem, then," he said, a smile slowly forming. "Why not bring a couple changes of clothes here, just for weekday moments like this. I think we both need these mid-week diversions."

"You may have hit upon the solution," she answered instantly. She surprised herself with the ease she accepted the idea. She really was undergoing a transformation.

And much to her surprise, she liked it.

Chapter 47

"Are they dangerous?" Alex's hand tightened around Blake's as she whispered in his ear.

"I doubt it, love," he whispered back, never taking his eye off the line of what appeared to be random creatures and mutant humans waiting to get into the Physics Café.

"Hey, you two," shouted a short guy with pointed ears. Blake thought he resembled an overgrown leprechaun in what appeared to be a uniform.

The leprechaun-like creature spoke again. "Get to the back of the line."

The others in the line grumbled as well.

"Then again, I may have misjudged the potential for hostility in this situation." By this time, he had his hand on the knob of the left door of the double set entering into the café.

As he scanned the long line, he realized many of the "things" standing in line had pointed ears. He got a better look at the uniforms as well. It seemed there was just one type. It was blue and from the quick survey of those wearing them, they were only properly worn if they were skin tight. On the left shoulder the garb sported a triangular emblem.

Still, a third, he guessed, appeared to be a strange hybrid between a werewolf and Bigfoot.

He tried to guide Alex inside, using the free door.

He could feel she was growing increasingly nervous. His movement into the coffee shop only excited the strange alien-like creatures more. The rumbling down the line grew louder and more formidable. Several creatures, evidently determined not to let them cut in, took several brisk steps in their direction.

"Excuse me, good man," he said, as calmly as he could gather. Only the bouncing of his hair belied his nervousness. He tried hard not to alarm Alex. "I do believe you're in our way."

Alex now quickly removed her hand from his and placed her arm around his waist. Things appeared to be going from bad to worse. The aliens began shouting. More than half a dozen of the uniformed individuals and hybrid creatures blocked their way.

The growing unrest finally caught Alvin's attention. He appeared at the door seemingly out of nowhere. "It's okay, guys," he told the creatures. "They're employees. They aren't going to drink the last Dark Hole Mocha or eat the last Philadelphia Experiment Cheesesteak."

Alvin them escorted them in. "The crowd is getting seriously restless out there. Sorry about that."

Blake and Alex followed Alvin through the café. Creatures resembling those outside occupied every table and booth. Their sheer numbers set him on edge. Not sure of their intention, he maintained a hold on Alex and deliberately kept pace with Alvin.

"This Space Cosplay Day is not only generating income," Alvin said, "But I've already had several newspaper reporters and a television station in here covering the event. And it's all due to your spontaneous text marketing plan. Me and the guys can't thank you enough."

As they passed one booth, a pair of werewolf-like creatures were getting up to leave. "Here, grab this booth before anyone else finds it. I'll be back in a second to clean it off."

The pair slid in, Alex rummaging through her backpack; Blake's eyes fixated on the television.

"I'm more confused than ever," he said. "When we were texting the event, I didn't understand what it was all about."

He paused, distracted by the action on the television across from them. "I'm still not sure I do." His eyes remained riveted on the television. "How about you? Is this an American thing that we Brits don't comprehend?"

The question was met with silence. He took his eyes off the television long enough to see Alex pull her history books out of her backpack. She surveyed the crowd before she answered.

"To be honest, I never really thought about what we were marketing. I just assumed you knew. But I never would have imagined it would look anything like this."

She took a second look around the café. A small smile crept on her face. "This may sound odd, but I feel strangely bonded to these creatures."

She pointed to a table across the room. "Watch those two over there. That's the strangest game of chess I've ever seen."

He looked behind him to a corner of the café. A gleaming crystal board and game pieces consisted of several levels. There were three conventional chess boards, stacked, step-like, atop one another. There were also four smaller boards, each with only four squares. Each player had another pair of boards that somehow hung in front of them on still another level. It was all very confusing.

His curiosity was aroused. He rose. "I'll be right back, love. I promise." He walked over to the players and stood just close enough to hear their conversation.

"Fascinating," said one as the other scooted a pawn over a spot. Then he deftly maneuvered one of his pieces without much thought.

A third person, also wearing the popular skin-tight costume, approached the table. He sipped his coffee as he leaned in closer and tilted his head.

"Any suggestions, doctor, as to how I may get myself out of this?" the one man asked and smiled up at him.

"Damn it, Jim," he said, "I'm a doctor not a chess player." Then he turned on a heel.

"I always wanted to use that line," he said, as he walked off.

Blake returned to find Alvin had bused the booth and Alex was already doing her homework, so he turned his attention to the television again.

"Look, love." He pointed to what he had been watching. He sat on his side of the booth, with one elbow resting on the table. "Those things on the screen do bear a faint resemblance to the werewolves or whatever sitting here before us. And look, they almost look like that one, too."

He pointed at another hybrid werewolf-Bigfoot creature who walked past as he munched on a plate of the Onion String Theory appetizer.

Alvin walked over with their lattes. "Look at all these characters," he said.

"So, everyone at the café," Alex asked as she took several pens out of her backpack, "are really characters from the television show?"

"Yeah, they are."

A character walked up to Alvin, separated his fingers, two on either side and greeted him, "Live long and prosper." Alvin returned the sign and the greeting.

"Gotta go," he said, "You want your usual Fission Chips, Blake?" Blake nodded vigorously. It always reminded him of home.

"Could I have a cup of your Primordial Soup and half a Chicken Time Warp Wrap?" Alex asked.

"Anything for the two best marketers in all of space-time continuum," Alvin said.

"So all these people in here today are misplaced characters from the TV series," Blake said after Alvin left.

Chapter 48

Alex dropped her pen and forgot about her homework. "I get it. I finally understand what this is all about."

Blake stared at her. "Great. Do you care to share?"

"All of these characters are trying to get home, just like us." Alex looked around, amazed at how many lost characters there were.

She jumped up and rushed over to the chess game.

"Excuse me, gentlemen, are you trying to get back to your world, too?" The three layers of the glass chess boards shimmered. One of the men had just made a move.

"Fascinating," the one with the pointed ears commented. "But not good enough, Jim." He moved another chess piece; she noticed it was a horse.

"Excuse me." She tried again. "I understand you're misplaced television characters who are trying to find a way back to your series. Is that true?"

The other man was about to make a move from the center board. He knitted his brow. "For the life of me, I don't know what you're talking about. This was the only costume left in my size on short notice at the party shop."

"Oh, you can tell me," she said. "I'm from a romance novel myself, and I'm trying to get back to the pages of my book."

"Fascinating," said the other man, "but highly

illogical."

She sighed and returned to the booth to find Blake eating his Fission Chips and watching the television. "Nobody's talking," she sighed.

"Can't blame them, love," Blake said, as he picked up a fry. "After all, we certainly haven't told anyone."

"You're right." She pursed her lips. "Of course. Now, why didn't I think of that?"

She tried to eat, but she found she had lost her appetite, as she thought about the café full of characters—all stranded in this world. *What chance do we have?*

"Do you think…" She turned to Blake, but he seemed oblivious to everything but the television show. She looked to see what held his attention.

She saw a man alone on a barren planet. He opened what looked like a flip cell phone and said, "Beam me up." No sooner than he uttered those words, he began to vanish.

Then the show cut to the next scene which showed him reappearing—particle by particle—on the spacecraft.

"Too bad we can't do that," Alex said. She knew she was whining, but she was truly homesick for the pages of her own book.

"That's it, love." Blake's outburst startled Alex. "You're a genius."

"I am? What did I say?"

"Come on, we've got a de-particlizer to operate." He grabbed her by the arm and headed for the kitchen area. He peeked in.

"Everyone is busy filling orders and the de-particlizer isn't being used. This is our chance to get home."

This is the man I love, she thought, as he rapidly explained the plan to her. *My hero.* She loved everything about him, from his unruly hair to his thoughtfulness.

She nodded her readiness. Her body tingled with excitement. *Home, finally.*

He took her hand and led her very quietly into the kitchen. She was astounded at the flurry of activity. He directed her attention to a small table that held a large gun.

"That's it," he whispered. "Our ticket home."

He lifted the gun above their heads and as he pulled the trigger, they said, "Beam us home." Nothing happened.

"I didn't feel a thing," she whispered. "Are you sure you pulled the trigger?"

"Yes. I pulled the trigger. Let's try again."

She took a deep breath. *This has got to work.*

"Stop! Are you out of your mind?" Alvin's voiced boomed and she jumped. She felt tears stream down her cheeks.

"This is piece of sensitive scientific equipment—not a toy." He grabbed the gun from Blake. "What do you think you're doing?"

"Just trying to get home." Alex kicked the leg of the table and ran out. Pushing her way through the throng of characters, she got back to their booth and shoved her belongings into her backpack.

She pushed her way through the crowd. She couldn't leave fast enough.

"Hey, lady," she heard someone say, "your backpack's open. You're going to lose all your books."

I don't care. I don't give a damn.

She found herself on the sidewalk and felt the presence of Blake before she saw him. He snatched the backpack from her, closed it, and swung it over his shoulder. "I'm sorry that didn't work. I thought it was a sure deal."

She stopped and looked into his deep chocolate-brown eyes. They were sincerely sad. Tears streamed down her face. "It's not your fault, honey. I'm just so frustrated. All I want is to get back to the pages of our story already. Is that really too much to ask?"

She paused a beat. "That really did sound like a guaranteed way."

He wrapped his arm around her small waist. She took a deep breath, whimpered, moved in a little closer, and placed her head on his shoulder.

"Thank you for trying. Let's just go to JJ's now. I could use some time away from all those creatures and mutants. I want to lock myself in the bedroom and have a good cry."

****

When JJ arrived home, she found Alex sulking on the couch. *She's not even studying her psychology,* she thought. *That's her favorite class.* She sat on the recliner next to the couch.

"Want to talk about it?" JJ asked quietly.

Alex turned to her and took a deep breath. "Why didn't you tell me Blake and I weren't the only lost characters in your world? How could you keep that from us? We're never going home, are we?"

Whoa. Now there was a lot to process. She took a deep breath and asked her to explain what other out-of-place characters she'd discovered.

She wanted to laugh when Alex finished her tale.

But as she looked at her character in tears, she realized the scenario was all too real for Alex.

Thankfully, Blake had just bounced into the room. "The pep squad and cheerleaders need us." He stopped in his tracks when he saw his love in distress. He hurried to her side and wrapped an arm around her.

"What's wrong, love?"

"That stupid de-particlizer didn't work," she sobbed.

JJ decided to take control of the situation. She couldn't have Alex in a forever-funk. "Listen to me, Alex Zurich. You're going to that cheerleaders meeting. As long as you're stuck in this world, you might as well interact with people."

Either the tone or the advice startled Alex and she immediately stopped sobbing.

"This advice comes from one who has spent too many years avoiding the world." She gave her character what she hoped was a stern look.

"And in the meantime, I have a theory of my own on how to get you two back to your book."

Alex's mood brightened immediately. "You do? What is it?"

Even Blake seemed surprised. "Can you share the details with us? Does it require any participation on our part?"

She feared she spoke too soon. It was only a theory. A very tentative one, at that. But, hell, when you're navigating unexplored territory like she had been for the last couple of months, any idea seems just as good as the next.

"No, it doesn't require the two of you to do anything. But it may take a while to work out. So, why don't you use your time here wisely and enjoy your friends and your classes knowing that you'll eventually get home?"

"That's so awesome, JJ." Alex jumped off the couch, leaving Blake sitting alone looking quite perplexed. She took a step toward JJ and bent over and gave her a bear hug. "I should have known you had a plan for us all along. You always have in the past."

She paused. "You remember that time when I thought Blake forgot about our date," she started.

She didn't and apparently that fact was clearly written all over her face.

"Page eighty-eight. You know, he was so late I thought he broke up with me and forgot to tell me."

She didn't know a person's countenance could change so dramatically in just a short time.

She pivoted. "Come on, Blake," she said, pulling him from the couch. "We can't be late."

Blake waved with his free arm as Alex dragged him through the living room.

"I pray this idea works," she whispered, as she headed for her office to write.

Chapter 49

Blake didn't know what JJ had up her sleeve, but he was relieved to hear she had plans to return them to their book. It took the burden of devising any more plans off of him. He admitted his plans had been nothing more than schemes. Ill-thought-out schemes, he admitted. The one aspect of this new world he would never be comfortable with was failure. He had failed the love of his life. More than once.

He was grateful that JJ had stepped in and helped. It was good to see Alex more content in their surroundings, just knowing that she would get home. That made every moment with her that much more delightful. Like now.

Blake sat next to her in what they had come to call "their booth." They chatted about the upcoming football game.

"It's the big one, from what I gather," he said. "It's the homecoming game."

"All the cheerleaders are talking about it," Alex said, her eyes twinkling. "I hear they pick a king and queen."

She paused as if she were thinking about it. "Justin and Sarah. They have my vote."

Blake was about to answer when it felt as if the floor were moving and he heard a loud rumble. That could only mean one thing.

"Earthquake!" Blake bolted from the booth, stood in

the aisle, and alerted everyone. "That shaking. It's an earthquake."

Alex ran next to him and gently whispered something in his ear. "It's a tornado, folks. Tornadoes are in Ohio. Duck and cover." Then he dove headfirst under the booth.

The rumbling, at first, was distant, yet distinct, then built quickly to a crescendo, and then became so loud that it was difficult to talk over it. An electric buzz of subdued conversation filled the café.

Then abruptly the noisy vibration ended. He felt the hair on the back of his neck raise. He waited for the tornado to hit. But it didn't.

"Look at that!" a customer said. "I've never seen so many motorcycles in my life."

He watched as every customer ran to the ceiling-to-floor windows to look at the scene. Alex came out from under the booth first and offered him a hand. Warily, he took it and crawled out.

His curiosity got the better of his fear. *What the bloody hell? I want to see this.* He sprinted over to join the crowd.

He called Alex to follow him. By the time she arrived, he was leaning against the far wall, adjacent to the window. Alex tucked herself in snugly in front of him. He wrapped his arms around her, and she clasped her hands over his wrists.

So, that's what the noise was? At least one, and sometimes two, motorcycles occupied every parking spot in front of the café.

"Those aren't just motorcycles," said a customer, "those beauties are all hogs. Sweet." He let out a low whistle.

Then as if on some invisible cue, the bikers dismounted. By this time, even Alvin had abandoned his post at the register to observe the commotion.

"I sure hope they don't plan to come in here," he said, "I don't need that kind tearing up the place."

A sea of black leather flooded the sidewalk. Tight-fitting chaps, leather vests, black T-shirts. It appeared that every single inch of the sidewalk was covered by this costumed group.

Then, in what appeared to be a well-rehearsed synchronized motion, the group pulled off their helmets.

"Ooh!" "Wow!" "Oh, my goodness." Disbelief and shock bubbled throughout the café as everyone caught their first glimpse of the faces of the motorcycle gang. White hair, white beards, white mustaches contrasted sharply with the black of the apparel. A few women were in the group, but most of them were gray as well. Only one or two of them were young enough to still have color in their hair.

"They're old people," a student commented. "Do you think there's one of them who's younger than sixty-five?"

"They're too old to be riding those things," someone else said.

"What a waste of a good machine," said another.

The sea of black leather and white hair began to swirl, like eddies on an ocean. The cyclists formed small groups, greeting each other, mingling, exchanging handshakes and high fives.

After several minutes, the eddies coalesced into a tide, headed straight for the coffee shop's door.

"Oh my! They're coming in here!" Immediately the customers ran back to their seats. The shop bristled with the sound of papers rustling, books closing and backpacks zipping. Most of them wanted out—as quickly as possible.

****

Alex beat Blake to the booth, and they both watched in fascination as the overage gang strode into the shop. Alvin hastily returned to the register, barely beating the first of the group to the counter.

"What an interesting phenomenon," Blake said.

Alex couldn't take her eyes off the bikers, as some lined up to place orders, while others went to secure seating.

Slowly, as orders were filled, the cascade of bikers filtered throughout the café, joining others at tables already claimed or looking for available booths, tables, or counter spaces.

Finally with every space filled, one couple was left. They wandered past Blake and Alex's booth unable to find a place to sit, he carrying the drinks and the order number placard.

"Excuse me, sir," Blake said as they passed, "you're more than welcome to join us if you'd like." Alex passed him a quick do-you-know-what-you're-doing glance. He nodded confidently in return.

The gentleman had a thick white head of hair, immediately giving the impression he was at least in his sixties. But his eyes shone a brilliant steel blue and his face, nearly wrinkle-free except for a few laugh lines around his eyes, making it difficult to determine his age. He nodded in reply and then deferred to his younger female companion.

His companion—much younger than he—was dressed in clunky black boots, snug black leather pants, a tight V-neck shirt, and a leather jacket. Alex thought she looked like a biker chick. Of course, she wasn't quite sure she knew what one looked like, having never encountered one before.

She did wonder, though, if this female had been poured into her outfit, sighing as she admitted she looked molten-lava hot. She darted her eyes in Blake's direction to assess his reaction. Wide-eyed, he stared open-mouthed. *Was he actually drooling?*

The amply endowed female had her hands shoved in the pockets of the jacket. Waving the jacket open and closed, she said, "I'd love to."

The man slid in next to Blake, placing his number on the table, and placed the woman's drink in front of her. The woman took Alex's side of the booth.

"Garrett," the biker immediately announced, "Garrett Shepherd. This is Rain." Garrett shook hands with Blake while Alex and Rain did the same.

"What an interesting name, Rain," Alex said.

"It's actually an acronym for all my names." She shrugged off her leather jacket and let it fall between her and the booth. "It stands for Renee April Indigo Nevada."

"Oh, uhm, different," Blake commented. Alex gently kicked his leg.

"I love it," Alex said, sipping on her quark flavored proton smoothie, a blend of kiwi and strawberry.

"Yeah, my parents were fascinated with the hippie life, even though they were a little young for it. They missed that whole scene by quite a few years. You might describe them as free spirits. So, they gave me a unique-sounding group of names. I turned it into Rain."

"Sounds like you might enjoy that free-spirit attitude

yourself," Blake said.

"Well, I must admit, I like surprising people. I enjoy breaking stereotypes."

"Rain and I are headed for Sturgis for the motorcycle rally," Garret said.

"Wow. Bike Week in Sturgis, South Dakota. I hear that event is amazing," Blake said. Alex wondered what it would be like to get on a motorcycle with the love of her life and just take off to, well, anyplace. The wind in their hair. The breeze slapping their cheeks. The bugs splattering their faces. She'd have to think about that road trip more.

"We're not going to South Dakota. We're a group of professional businessmen—CEOs, CFOs, bank presidents, upper-level management. We can't take the time off from work to ride all the way out to South Dakota." He paused and took a sip of his drink.

"Heck, at our ages, I don't think we'd even survive the trip all the way there."

"But you said you were going to Sturgis." Alex's curiosity piqued.

"Sturgis, Indiana," Rain said. "It's a lot closer and they do a great job of holding a mini-rally for bikers. It's really lots of fun—without that excruciatingly long trip for those of us east of the Mississippi."

"5B."

"That's our food. I'll be right back." Garrett headed toward the counter.

"You two make such a cute couple," Alex told Rain, as she cupped her hands around her drink.

Rain placed her hand on Alex's forearm. "No, we're not a couple in that sense." She released her hand and angled her body so it was more favorable to a one-on-

one conversation.

"I'm traveling with Garrett and the group as part of a sociology study I'm conducting. I've been fascinated by this group for the longest time. I finally received a chance to study them. I'm documenting this event for my research for my doctoral dissertation."

"Something like Jane Goodall and the chimpanzees," Blake said.

Alex kicked his legs. "Blake."

"Ouch." He reached down and rubbed his leg.

"That's okay," Rain said, her eyes dancing as she looked at Alex, who was re-evaluating her initial reaction to her based on her clothing.

"You'd be amazed how often I'm compared to her."

"Darn, I'm not original."

Garrett returned with their food. He gave Rain her Chernobyl Chicken Meltdown.

"Despite the name, it sounded good," she said, as if she felt she had to explain her choice.

Garrett placed his Schrodinger's Steak on the table in front of him and eyed it.

"I've seen steak served in all types of ways, but I've never seen one served under a box, like this. Are they trying to hide something?"

"The box represents the thought experiment of Erwin Schrodinger," Blake explained, "created to illustrate the paradox of quantum superposition."

"What?" Garrett evidently did not see the connection. Blake continued his explanation.

"How did you order your steak?" Blake placed the palm of his hand on the box.

"Medium well."

"In the thought experiment, Schrodinger also

envisioned a radioactive substance in the box with a cat."

"Wait, are you telling me this steak is radioactive." Garrett's eyes grew wide.

Alex couldn't help but giggle and felt compelled to allay the man's fears. "No, not at all."

Blake continued. "According to quantum physics, the unseen cat could be alive or dead, depending on the consciousness of the observer."

Garret now just looked puzzled. "Okay. But how does that relate to my steak?"

"Whether the cook prepared it medium well or not depends on your consciousness. Until you take the lid off, the steak could be done in any number of ways."

Alex beamed proudly at her boyfriend.

Garrett gave him a blank stare. "You mean my steak might not be medium well?"

"In all probability, no pun intended, it is. But, if by some chance, it isn't done as you wanted, it's the café's disclaimer." Blake paused, took a sip from his cup as Garrett stared at his plate. "Not to worry, they will make you another steak if your consciousness sees anything but how you ordered it."

"Go, ahead, Garrett," Rain said, placing her hand on the box. "We'll send an intention out into the Universe so your steak is medium well."

Garrett laughed, took a deep breath, then lifted the box, placing it to the side. He cut into the steak, examining its state. "Ah, just the right hint of pink. Medium well."

But the biker stared at his plate. "What's up with these mashed potatoes? They're shaped a little strange."

Alex giggled, again. "Those are called Devil's Tower potatoes. They were inspired from the movie about aliens, where that character sculpted his mashed potatoes to look like that." Garrett just shook his head, as he picked up his fork.

"So, what's your story?" Rain asked Alex, before taking a bite of her meltdown.

"Love's Surprise." Alex said spontaneously, providing her with the title of the book they had bounded out of.

"I beg your pardon."

"What she means is you'd be surprised by it," Blake said hastily. "We're originally from Kansas, but staying with a cousin of Alex's while we…"

Alex knew he was about to say make our way home, so she helped him out.

"…work on our degrees. We've only recently enrolled in UNO. After we graduate, we'll probably go back home to Kansas."

The two couples continued to chat. Rain took the last sip of her smoothie, then put her leather jacket on. "Garrett, I'll meet you at the hotel in a couple hours. I'm going to check in on that old friend of mine I was telling you about."

Garrett stood. "Thank you for your hospitality," he said, "hopefully, we'll run into each other before we leave."

"We have to leave, too," Alex said. "We told JJ we'd drop by and visit her."

Chapter 50

Kenn looked at the caller ID on his phone and sighed. His mother. He was at the office, absorbed in grading his half of the conspiracy class term papers.

He didn't have the time or energy to deal with her.

He ran a hand through his hair, as he briefly contemplated not answering it. But he knew the extent of his mom's tenacity. She would only call the office and Deb would put her through. *Might as well get this out of the way now.*

"Hi, Mom."

"Are you and JJ still together? I haven't heard from you in a long time. I'm worried."

He rose from his chair and rubbed his neck. "Yes, Mom. We're still together."

"That's a relief. Do you think she's the one? I'm hoping she's the one."

How the hell do I answer that? Of course, JJ was the one. He knew that the first time he saw her at the bookstore. He also knew that someday soon he would propose. He thought about JJ all the time. But he couldn't tell his mom that. He didn't want to tell her that. That wasn't a conversation you have with your mother.

"I really don't have time to discuss this right now. I'm in the middle of grading papers."

He glanced to his left and looked at the stack of papers on the floor; he still had a lot to get through. He didn't need this distraction.

"I'm just saying she's a lot better choice than the last one you dated. What was her name? I knew it just the other day."

"Rain!" He had heard the knock at the door. And there she stood.

"That was it," his mother said.

"Mom, I've got to go." And he ended the call and stood.

"Rain, what a surprise." He swallowed hard when he saw his former girlfriend, dressed in a skin-tight T-shirt and black leather jacket.

She ran up to him, embraced him, and planted a kiss on his unsuspecting lips. He resisted as she tried to maneuver him.

"Rain, what the hell are you doing?" He hoped she understood him, because her lips wouldn't let go of his.

"I've missed you, honey. I want to get back together."

He understood the words only too well. He tried to separate himself from her, but she was amazingly strong for such a small person. As he squirmed to get out of her grip, he lost his balance and fell on the pile of term papers and took Rain down with him. She lay there without apparently making an effort to get up.

****

"I know he's been busy grading papers practically nonstop," JJ told Alex and Blake as they walked to Kenn's office. "I bet he can use a Physics Café break."

"What the hell is going on? Who the hell is she?" JJ pointed at the woman dressed in biker apparel.

"JJ, meet—" Blake began.

Alex bopped him on the back of the head.

"What?" Blake rubbed his head.

The woman jumped up and adjusted her T-shirt.

"This must look horrible," Kenn said, as he tried to climb his way out of the mess of midterm essays. His companion looked startled.

JJ marched toward the two and shoved the woman out of her way to get closer to Kenn. The woman lost her balance and tried to grasp the desk to break her fall. It proved useless. She toppled to the floor.

"What the hell do you think you're doing?" the woman said. She ignored her as she glared at Kenn.

Once again, Blake tried to introduce the two, but Alex stopped him. "Well, they haven't been properly introduced."

Kenn finally got to his feet. That allowed JJ to get into his face. Well, as close to his face as she could, considering the height difference.

"What were you doing? Who is this…this…" She glanced at the other woman and finally decided on a nondescript term. "…person?"

Involuntary tears swelled in her eyes. Her breathing became shallow. She glared. She opened her mouth to say something but realized no words could express the pain in her heart. She slapped him in the face, turned on a heel, and dashed out of the office.

She had no idea where she was headed; she just wanted to get as far away from that man as quickly as possible.

"Come on, Blake," she heard Alex say, "we've got to follow her."

She wanted to be alone. For the rest of her life.

Chapter 51

"Go away," JJ said when she saw Alex and Blake. She was already working on her second latte. Confused, bewildered, and feeling betrayed after what she witnessed, she wasn't sure where to turn.

She stopped momentarily at her office, but it was too small to contain her anger. She didn't want to go home. Not yet, at least. She needed a neutral location where she could think things out.

Okay, so perhaps the Physics Café wasn't that neutral of a location considering the amount of time she had spent there with that man. But it beat out every other place. Besides, here she could drown herself in coffee.

She just wanted to be alone. That was why having her creations standing in front of her was so annoying. Against her better judgment, she signaled for them to sit down.

Just at that moment, Dr. Chare and Rain walked in. JJ's eyes widened and her muscles tensed.

"Now, that little witch is hitting on Professor Chare. Trying to break up another relationship. How many is she shooting for in one day?"

She chugged the rest of her drink and pushed the mug away from her.

"And to think, I let myself fall in love with Kenn." She looked across the table at Alex and Blake. They looked pretty woeful in their own way.

"See? This is what happens when you let someone into your heart in real life. Heartbreak." She shook her head. "Why did I ever listen to you two?"

She sighed and tried not to let her characters know there were tears welling up in her eyes. "I'm going to get another cup of coffee. I'll be right back."

"No, don't." Blake jumped up and grabbed the empty cup. "I'll get it for you. I have to get ours anyway."

She nodded. But that still meant she was left with Alex. "You should be happy you're a character in a book. Characters like you are bestowed with a unique privilege. They're ensured that their romance will end in a happily-ever-after."

She chastised herself for allowing Alex and Blake to lead her down a romantic path she felt she had no right to travel. "And do you know why you're endowed with that gift? Do you?"

She wanted Alex to understand just how much forethought and planning went into a novel, in particular the novel in which she was the heroine.

"I'll tell you why," she continued, not waiting for an answer. But she was interrupted by Blake's return with the three mugs of coffee.

"Here you go, JJ." Blake's cheerfulness rubbed her dour mood like sandpaper.

"Quit being so bright," she said. "I didn't bring my sunglasses. I can't take it."

Then she thanked him. "Now, where was I?"

"In the pit of despair?" Blake said as he sat down.

"Ouch, why did you kick me? She obviously is."

"That, too, but I was telling Alex while you were gone why you characters always find true love."

"Go ahead, JJ, I want to hear this," Alex said.

"Because the reader demands it. I spent hours upon hours on your plot, creating a storyboard that spanned the walls of my office. I placed and replaced both of you so you would be in exactly the right place at exactly the right time just so you, Alex"—she shook her finger at her heroine—"and you, Blake"—she wagged her finger at him, as well—"could have a happily-ever-after experience."

Huge tears streamed down her cheeks. Alex reached across the table and held her hand. No words were uttered for what seemed like a long moment.

"Buck up, Pilgrim." Blake finally broke the silence. "What makes you think you're at the end of your love story? In every great romance novel, there's always that moment of discouragement. Just when you think the hero and heroine are on the way to true love, something happens." He paused. "But then they always find a way to overcome it to reach their happily-ever-after. Always."

Blake took a sip of coffee. "And you should know that better than anyone."

The forceful words stung her. It was the last thing she expected. But evidently, Blake wasn't done.

"Instead of sitting here feeling sorry for yourself, go fight for Kenn's love. Isn't that what every heroine does? Go back to the History Department…"

She quit listening after "go fight for Kenn's love."

"Of course. Who the hell does she think she is, anyway? I can't let her get away with that?"

She jumped from her seat and scanned the café. Then she spotted exactly who she was searching for. She marched up to her and interrupted her conversation with

Dr. Chare.

"Hey, you," she said loudly enough for everyone in the café to stop whatever they had been doing.

"The name is Rain."

"I don't care if your name is Snow White, you've got to leave my boyfriend alone." She placed her hands on her hips.

Rain stood up, her eyes narrowed, meeting JJ's. Energized by caffeine and adrenaline, she took the other woman's stance as a physical challenge. She realized Rain was about four inches taller than her, but only because of the biker boots she wore. She calculated her chances of winning.

She certainly didn't allow any disadvantage on her part to stop her. She pulled the front of the woman's shirt, bringing Rain just a bit closer so she could stare into her eyes. Then she shouted in her face.

"I love Kenn Cooper. You need to butt out of my life. You're not in this portion of the novel anymore, babe. I'm writing this book. Go back to wherever you came from and find yourself someone else, anyone else."

She let go of Rain, who seemed to be shocked. Before the woman could recover, though, JJ pulled her by the shirt again. "Anyone but Dr. Chare. Cause he's way too nice for you. You even think about meddling with him, and I'll make you regret it."

JJ pushed Rain into the chair. The woman bounced off it and fell on the floor.

"This is beginning to get old," Rain said. "And I'm tired of it. And I'm tired of you. You're gonna pay, you little witch."

She shot up from the floor at lightning speed.

"What did you call me, you tramp?" JJ asked.

****

"Come on, Blake, we have to help JJ." Blake felt himself being pushed out the booth and led to the area where the two women were arguing. He intentionally kept a safe distance from them.

Dr. Chare jumped from his seat and strode over to them. He nudged Blake.

"The entertainment here is fascinating. But I can't stay for it. If I actually witness it, I'd have to reprimand someone. However, if I only receive the hearsay version, I don't have to believe it and, therefore, don't have to dole out any suspension."

He turned on a heel, then looked back. "Have a great time. This should prove very interesting." Blake watched as the professor beelined for the exit.

"I didn't know that old man could move that fast," he said, with a bit of awe.

"And this is for pushing me in Kenn's office," Rain said. His attention immediately returned to the argument.

Rain pushed JJ into a table where two coeds sat. They screamed and jumped as lattes splashed onto their designer jeans and sweaters. JJ lay there a moment. She watched as Rain approached, then pulled both legs back and used the leverage to push her into a booth several feet away.

The coffee that had been on that table splashed everywhere, and a plate of Feynman Fries with cheese flew into the air. The guys at the booth whistled.

JJ got to her feet and walked over. She looked down at Rain. "Kenn is off the market. Permanently, you witch."

He grinned. "What an adventure," he told Alex.

"Please tell me this wasn't what you had in mind

when you told JJ to go fight for Kenn's love," Alex said, sounding concern.

"Not quite. But you have to admit this is interesting."

The customers started cheering.

"My money's on JJ," said one student.

"Nope, that biker chick's going to knock the crap out of her." He watched as the man pulled out his wallet. "Here's a five. The biker girl wins."

His companion pulled out his own wallet and set a five-dollar bill down. "JJ. All the way."

He saw the crowd's increasing participation and couldn't resist the temptation. He ran to the area where the baristas worked, leapt over the counter, and took control of the microphone normally used to announce completed orders.

"JJ 'Micro Munchkin' Spritely has just taken a nasty fall." His words echoed throughout the café. "But wait. She's back on her feet, fire in her eyes, and hatred in her heart. And she's headed straight for Rain, the Heartbreak Kid."

The crowd reacted to his commentary, which only encouraged him. "Micro Munchkin grabs the Heartbreak Kid by the arm." He paused. "What's she doing now? No, no it doesn't appear she's going to throw the Heartbreak Kid down as you might expect."

His voice raised an octave as he excitedly reported on the details. His hair danced wildly to the movements of his head, which were coordinated with the action of the two women.

"No, she's biting her arm with all the tenacity of an English bulldog."

The loud, raucous approval of the crowd drowned

out Rain's cry of pain.

He watched in wonder as Rain wound up her right arm and drove it into JJ's eye. "Ouch," he winced into the microphone. The crowd groaned, as well.

He recovered quickly and resumed his duties. "The Heartbreak Kid just smashed her fist right into Micro Munchkin's eye."

He paused a moment, as he reveled in the full effect of the impromptu women's wrestling match. "That's gotta hurt, folks. You don't take a beating like that and walk away from it."

The punch knocked JJ flat on her butt. As she tried to pull herself up, Rain took hold of her arm and dragged her behind the bar. Blake had a clear view of what was happening even if the crowd didn't. He felt his duty to report it.

"The Heartbreak Kid is pouring coffee grounds on Micro Munchkin's head. Now, that's grounds for retaliation," he quipped, quite pleased with his humor.

He watched as a photographer for *The Daily Digit* ran up and snapped a photo.

"Ah, immortalized forever."

Chapter 52

JJ and Rain stood and glared at each other after the arresting officer pushed them into the same cell at the Bell Wyck Police Department.

"This is all your fault, you little slut," JJ said. She scanned the small setting. To call it sparse, she thought, was an understatement. A set of bunk beds sat in one corner with lumpy mattresses. In another corner were the sink and a toilet.

"That's right," said the man in the cell next to them, who hung on to the bars as he watched them.

She looked over and gave him what she hoped was a dirty look. It did nothing to deter him.

"My fault? Hardly. I wasn't doing anything but kissing my boyfriend."

"That's what she was doing," the onlooker said. She now knew, by the way he slurred his words, the man was in there for drunkenness.

"But he's my boyfriend now. I don't even know where you came from."

"Yeah, where did you come from, come to think of it?" the drunk asked, eyes squinted and head tilted.

"Shut up!" Rain and JJ said simultaneously and flashed him angry looks. Their spontaneous answer prompted them both to laugh. Rain turned and sat on the bed.

"I sure hope we don't have to spend the night here.

This mattress is paper thin."

JJ sat next to her. "How in the world did we even end up here?"

"You guys got arrested. Hell, I'm drunk and I even know that."

"Shut up!"

"He's right, you know," JJ said. "We got arrested." She paused. "Over a damned man." JJ kicked a leg.

"It's all my fault." Rain rose and faced JJ. "I'm sorry to get you into this mess." She tilted her head and smiled. "I bet if I took the time to get to know you, I'd really like you."

"No, it's my fault," JJ said. "I pushed you first. And I did bite you. You'll probably need a tetanus shot."

Rain laughed. "I'll be sure to get one. But you're going to have one nasty black and blue mark on that eye." She paused. "You had every right to shove and bite me. You see, I really was trying to come on to Kenn. I knew the bike group I was riding with was stopping in Bell Wyck. I had every intention of winning him back."

She knew she should be furious at hearing this, but something in Rain's eyes calmed her. Or maybe she was just tired of fighting.

"But for the first time, I couldn't persuade him. Before, I could always convince him that we were made for each other." She paused. "And it never mattered if he already had a girlfriend. I'm not proud of that. But there's something special about that man."

"Yes," JJ said, nodding slowly as she thought about him. "There is something special about him."

Rain smiled. "I didn't know you were even in the picture. He really didn't want anything to do with me. Honest." She crossed her heart.

JJ thought about the scene in his office. She now realized his squirming was an effort to put distance between them. "Did you see the horrified look on his face when he saw me?"

"I saw the look, but I didn't know what caused it." She laughed. "He looked scared shitless." She laughed, fueled in part by Rain's colorful description.

"He must really love you, that's all I can say."

She sat on the edge of the bunk and invited Rain to do the same. "Tell me about yourself. I want to get to know you better."

Soon the pair was comparing educational experiences in addition to anecdotes about Kenn.

"You should have seen his reaction," JJ said, "when he found out I was a romance author."

"You mean, you're that JJ Spritely? I've read your books. I love your work."

"Oh, yeah, now we're all lovey-dovey over there, aren't we?" the drunk said.

They laughed.

"It looks like you two have kissed and made up. How touching." JJ jumped off the bunk when she heard her sister's voice.

Nan glared at her; arms crossed. Rob stood behind her, smiling. Alex and Blake stood behind him.

"I have never been so embarrassed in my life," Nan said, even before checking to see if she was hurt. "What in the world were you thinking?"

Instead of answering, JJ turned to her cellmate. "This sister of mine moaned when she thought I didn't have a life of my own. And now that I do, she's still moaning. There's just no pleasing some people."

She returned her attention to Nan, whose pose

hadn't changed. The other three looked as if they were suppressing laughter.

Nan let out a dramatic sigh. "Getting a life doesn't mean getting yourself thrown in jail. And if I hadn't already paid that bond, I'd leave you in there for that remark."

Just then, a police officer walked toward the group, stepped in front of Nan, and unlocked the cell door.

"Come on out, both of you. You've been bonded out."

Rain looked astonished. "Who paid for my bail?"

"Some guy named Thomas Chare."

Rain broke into laughter. "What a delightful man he is."

They exited and JJ immediately rushed over to Alex and hugged her.

"Why does she get a hug?" Nan exploded. "I'm the one who paid for her bail."

"Calm down, dear," Rob said. "Let it go."

JJ pivoted. "Does anyone know where Kenn is?"

Rob raised a tentative hand. "I do." He glanced at his wife. "He texted me. He's at the Physics Café. He said he's drowning himself in cappuccinos at the barista bar."

"That's not a good sign," Rain said. "Come on"— Rain grabbed JJ's arm—"we better get over there, pronto."

As the women started down the hall, they bumped into Garrett who was jogging toward the cell. JJ noticed Dr. Chare not far behind him. Amazingly, he was trying to jog.

Garrett gave Rain a quick hug. "Are you all right? Your arm. It looks as if you got bitten."

"I did. But we'll talk about that later. Right now, I have to ask you a big favor."

"Of course. Anything."

"Meet JJ." The two shook hands. "Could you please give her a ride to the Physics Café? She's got a very important appointment that she can't be late for."

"What are we waiting for?"

"Aren't you coming too?" JJ asked.

"I'll be there, but right now it's more important that you get there first."

She paused. Dr. Chare was standing there, bent over breathing hard. "I'm sure Dr. Chare would be happy to give me a ride."

"Of course." The chair beamed. Even though he was still breathing heavily, he extended his right elbow out for Rain to take. They followed Garrett and JJ down the hall.

"Wait for us," Alex called. "Don't forget us."

"And me," Rob said. "I've got to see what happens next."

JJ heard his footsteps, just a bit faster than anyone else's.

"For crying out loud," Nan sighed, clearly irritated. "I guess I have to see this, too."

Chapter 53

JJ felt the wind ripping through her clothes. *It's not like I woke up this morning planning to ride on a motorcycle,* she thought. The chilly fall air proved downright cold when it hits you at fifty miles per hour, she observed. She swayed to the right and the left along with the cycle as Garrett navigated the potholes. *I'll never do this again. Speed may be of the essence, but I'd really love to live long enough to see Kenn again.*

Garrett shouted something back at her, momentarily taking his eyes off the road. Because of the rumble of the bike, the whooshing of the wind, and the protective helmet, his words reached her as mere garble. He didn't seem to notice as he immediately turned his head and concentrated on the road again.

Finally, the bike came to a halt in front of the Physics Café. It felt as if it went from fifty miles an hour to nothing in three seconds. First the motorcycle stopped, then her body stopped. But not before it bumped into Garrett's back.

Clumsily, she dismounted the cycle. No easy task for someone so short or so inexperienced in the act. She stumbled backward a few steps before regaining her balance. Getting off these things, she thought, looks so easy in the movies.

Once stable, she dashed into the café. Her only thought was her need to explain herself to Kenn. She

Terry Newman

couldn't lose him, not now. Now that she had learned how wonderful having a real life was—even with all of its ups and downs.

She found him exactly where Rob said he would be, at the barista bar, talking with Alvin.

"An enormous pompous ass." JJ heard his muffled admission.

"It's Micro Munchkin in the flesh," Alvin said. That's when she took a good look around. Several broken chairs were in one corner.

"Sorry about the fight. I'll pay for the damages." She looked at her feet. "It may take me a while."

"We'll discuss that later." He nodded in Kenn's direction.

"Kenn, we need to talk."

Immediately, he stood and assumed his self-defense pose of the Tai chi flamingo, left leg up, hands covering his face and his eyes tightly closed.

"Hey, Micro Munchkin," Alvin said. She took a deep breath. Her muscles tightened at being interrupted. "What?"

"Take off the helmet. You'll gain some credibility."

New to the whole helmet thing, she fumbled with the fastener for a moment. Finally, she removed it. With her expanded view, she was able to see more. And what she saw surprised her. The café was unusually full of customers, the vast majority of them students, of course. And it felt like every single one of them had their eyes trained on her.

Out of the corner of her eye, she saw Alex and Blake rush in. She also noticed that several members of the cheerleaders and pep squad immediately pulled them out. That was of little concern to her at the moment,

258

however.

She gave her full attention to Kenn. It looked as if every second it was increasingly more difficult for him to hold the pose. She could see him totter a bit. "Preparing for the worst, I see."

"Yes, ma'am. Just standing here waiting for you to unleash your unique brand of anger on me." He spread his fingers slightly and opened his eyes. She couldn't help but smile. *He's a very special man, all right.*

"Let's go outside," she said, still feeling the eyes of the students as they evidently waited for a floor show. She took his hand and led him through the café. A large collective groan echoed throughout the establishment.

The students watched them closely. Her cheeks grew hot in response, and she knew they were glowing crimson. Once safely out of earshot on the sidewalk, she poured out her feelings.

"Yes, I was furious when I saw the two of you on the floor like that. But I've come to understand the situation. It's difficult to spend time together in a six-by-nine jail cell as we did and not share some very personal, private moments."

"You were in jail? In the same cell as Rain?" He rolled his eyes.

"That's a story for another day. What I'm trying to say now is that your ex-girlfriend testified about your loyalty. The jealously, the insecurity I felt, that's all part of my problem." She paused. His chocolate-colored eyes looked down at her expectantly.

"Starting a new relationship, a new life, after all this time hasn't been easy." She sighed. "And it's been scary. Very scary."

"I understand, darling. I really do." He approached

her slowly. He gently placed his hands on her arms and gazed into her eyes. She swore her body sizzled when he touched her. If she had doubts she was making the right move, they evaporated.

"Believe me," he said, pulling her a little closer. "Rain seriously hurt me when she left. For a while I wasted so much time trying to 'replace' her. Then I saw you standing there in the bookstore. I knew you were not your average woman, but I acted like such a jerk."

She closed her eyes and shook her head as she remembered their first disastrous encounter.

"I didn't do much to help you out."

He pulled her closer, his eyes meeting hers. Her spine tingled as she studied his boyish face, a face she now knew so well; she knew every laugh line.

He placed his hand on her neck and pulled her even closer, their lips met, and they were lost in the moment, a very long sensual moment. Slowly their lips parted but the embrace lingered.

"I swore when I kissed you, I heard music and angels singing."

"Of course, you did." She nestled into his warm sensuous body. "It's the homecoming parade. The music is the marching band, and the angels are the cheerleaders."

The float with the homecoming king and queen was directly in front of them. On it were Alex and Blake, arms wrapped around each other, waving. "Look who made the royalty." Kenn chuckled.

"Yay, JJ! You and Kenn got back together," Alex shouted.

"Now that's a happily-ever-after," Blake said and winked.

She and Kenn waved. Alex turned to Blake and kissed him passionately. The crowd roared with delight and applauded.

"That's our cue," he softly told her. He tightened his embrace. She closed her eyes, soaking in the exquisite moment. When the crowd noise around them reached a crescendo, she slowly opened one eye and glanced at the café. The windows were lined with students, applauding and cheering.

"I do believe we have an ever-expanding audience," she mumbled.

"Well, then let's give them something they can remember."

Chapter 54

"So exactly what happens to me at the end of my book?"

Alex sat on the couch in the study, legs crossed at the knee, her hands cupped around the top one.

JJ had finished *Love's Surprise* and was printing it out before she sent the digital to her editor.

While she didn't need to send the physical manuscript to her publisher, she had gotten into the habit of saving a hard copy for herself. She never hit the send button on her email until she had her copy printed and secured in a sturdy box.

She even had a section of her bookshelf dedicated to the manuscripts. It was an oddly satisfying habit.

When she didn't answer, Alex continued her line of questioning.

"Or am I going to have to wait until the book is published to discover how my love unfolds?" Alex paused. JJ looked up from her packing and saw the sorrow in her character's eyes.

"Am I going back home any time soon?" Her voice cracked.

Alex uncrossed her legs, scooted to the edge of the loveseat, and covered her eyes. JJ recognized the mixture of sadness and anger in her and abandoned her task to sit with her. She could see Alex's stomach quickly rise and fall with every silent sob.

"Don't cry, sweetheart," JJ said. "You'll get back, I'm sure."

"When? How?" Tears finally broke through and streamed down her cheeks. "I thought once we got you and Kenn securely together we'd somehow be magically transported back to our book. Just like we were magically transported here. But look at me, I'm still stuck in this God forsaken place."

Alex gasped and grabbed JJ's hand. "I'm so sorry. You know I didn't mean that. You've been a wonderful friend."

She wasn't sure how to handle the situation. It's not like she was an expert in comforting fictional characters trapped in the real world. Though, on second thought, she probably was the one author who had the most experience.

She pushed those errant thoughts from her head and refocused on Alex's obvious pain.

"I know you didn't mean it. And you know what? It's okay even if you did."

JJ placed her hand over Alex's. "It's not your home. I understand your frustration and your loneliness. Trust me, I never thought you and Blake would be here this long, either."

Even though they had frustrated her initially, the thought of living in her world without them saddened her. She had come to love them. She appreciated their enthusiasm and their concern for her wellbeing. And she even grew to love and appreciate Blake's humor. *What would life be like without them?*

As if on cue, Blake bounced in, carrying a tray with three cups of freshly brewed coffee. His broad smile faded when he saw Alex.

Hastily, he looked at the desk, obviously searching for an empty spot to put the tray. Between the box for the manuscript and other papers there was no room. Sensing his dilemma, JJ jumped up and moved the box to the credenza behind her desk.

Blake laid the tray down and hurried over to Alex.

"I want to go home. I want to go home, now," she pleaded.

JJ picked up two of the cups and quickly handed one to Alex.

"Here, hon. Maybe this will help."

"This one's for you, Blake."

He took the cup but kept one arm tenderly around her shoulders. "Love, we'll get back, I promise. I know I haven't been able to make it happen yet, but, I promise, I'll find a way."

Alex looked into his eyes. JJ wondered what she was thinking. Then with a slight smile, she thought, I know how I would script this scene. *Alex gazed into his brown eyes and saw the soul within the man. In those kind eyes, she saw a man who enjoyed every moment of life, who laughed heartily, loved fiercely. A man who would die for her. She saw the one and only man she would ever love.*

Alex spoke slowly, trying hard to control her sobs. "You've been so wonderful. You've tried everything. It's not your fault. There's a missing puzzle piece that we just can't seem to find yet." She paused. "And it's infuriating."

She decided her help wasn't needed at the moment, so she returned to her task. She was ready to print the final chapter of the book.

JJ hit the print button on the computer and took a sip

of coffee while the printer did its thing.

When the printer stopped, she placed the cup on the tray, retrieved the pages, and arranged them in its proper place in the manuscript. Finally, every page was printed. She sighed contently as she closed the box.

"The novel is officially completed." JJ glanced at Alex and Blake, but they were engaged in their own problem. She pulled the email up and hit the send button.

"Your love story to be exact," she further explained as she turned to look at them again. But the fictional characters were gone. The loveseat was empty.

"That's odd."

"What is?" She looked up to see Kenn leaning against the doorjamb, one leg casually crossed over the other. He held two cups, one bright yellow, the other cobalt blue.

She glanced at the desk. It held no tray or coffee cups.

"There was a tray…" She stopped in midsentence. She looked at the loveseat, again. It was still empty. Slowly she smiled, then everything clicked. So that really was their mission here, she thought. To make sure I began living my own life. Silently she congratulated them. She broke into laughter.

"What's so funny?" He walked into the room, offering her the yellow cup. "French roast coffee, sweetheart. Your favorite."

She took the cup, inhaled the marvelous aroma. "I always get a little giddy when I complete a novel, that's all. There's a part of me that just can't believe my good fortune."

"Good fortune, bull," Kenn said. "You've got talent, both as a historian and a romance author. And I'm the luckiest guy in the world to have you in my life."

His eyes pierced her soul. Her knees buckled.

"Congratulations, sweetheart. I propose a toast."

They both held their cups up. "To happily ever after."

Clanking their mugs, she repeated, "To happily ever after."

A word about the author...

Terry Newman has always loved words. As the editor-in-chief of a national natural health publishing company, she has written books on a variety of topics, as well as writing direct-mail advertising.

She's also worked as a reporter, a communications specialist, and a freelance writer. She'd had clients worldwide and researched and wrote hundreds of eBooks and print books as well as ghostwrote novellas and short stories.

One day she woke and decided to make her dream of writing her own novel come true. She sets all her stories in fictional towns in northeast Ohio and writes about things she loves—like coffee.

Terry has taught workshops on writing and character development.

She has a daughter, a son-in-law, and a grandpuppy, and lives in North Lima, a real town in northeast Ohio.

www.terrynewmanauthor.com

Thank you for purchasing
this publication of The Wild Rose Press, Inc.

For questions or more information
contact us at
info@thewildrosepress.com.

The Wild Rose Press, Inc.
www.thewildrosepress.com